BLOOD BOND
SKIN TRADE

MASON SABRE

DARK WOLF BOOKS

Blood Bond

Mason Sabre

This book is a work of fiction. All characters in this novel are fictitious. Any resemblance to actual events or locales or persons, living or dead, is entirely coincidental.

Author: Mason Sabre

Copyright © 2023 by Mason Sabre. All rights reserved, including the right to publish this book or portions thereof (except for reviews, news media reports, brief quotes with attribution, and purposes of promotion of this book or other novels by Mason Sabre in any form whatsoever.

Written permission may be obtained from the author.

PLACES TO FIND ME

Mason Sabre

Email me - masonsabre2@gmail.com

Find me on facebook - https://www.facebook.com/msabre3

Website – Masonsabre.com

My author page - https://www.facebook.com/AuthorMasonSabre

Also by Mason Sabre

Society Books

Book 1 Cade

Book 2 Dark Veil

Book 3 Case 36

Book 4 Hidden

Book 5 Fractured

Book 6 Sebastian

Book 7 Exile

Book 8 Broken

Book 9 The Forgotten

Origin story - The Rise of the Phoenix

Origin Story - Henry

Book 10 Moon Night

Book 11 Alpha - Coming soon

Society Companion Books

Death Awakening

Broken Snow

Seraph

Bleed

Chaos

Martial Magic

Enigma

Mortal Wings

Fangliner

Rogue

Other Books by Mason Sabre

Death Dealers (With Rachel Morton)

Dead on Time

Dead on Arrival

Dead on Target

Dead to Me

Skin Trade Series

Blood Slave

Blood Oath

Blood Bond

Others

Watch Over you

Cuts Like an Angel

Cuts like an Angel 2

Cuts Like an Angel 3

Lucy

She Promised

Twisted

Non-Fiction

10,000 Words per Day

Write Better Scenes

Patreon for Writers

TEAM SABRE

Wolf Club

Help me to keep these books coming by joining my Patreon. In return, I'll give you exclusive access to chapters before the books are released, a behind the scenes look at my writer life and not published elsewhere short stories.

I also give away advanced copies of books in ebook format before they're released as well as signed paperbacks, hardbacks, mugs, and other merchandise at no extra cost to you. It is all part of your support.

But not just that. You'll be joining an already thriving reader community, where I get to chat with you about the books you love to read.

Support from $3 and you can cancel anytime you like, with no questions. But I'm pretty sure you won't want to.

See you there.

Mason

https://www.patreon.com/masonsabre

CHAPTER
ONE

I'm in Seth's arms, locked in a death grip as we soar through the sky. The world around us blurs into a sickening haze, and the ground below has transformed into an abyss of terrifying shadows, rising to swallow us whole. My heart pounds like thunder in my chest. "We have to go back. Please..." I reach for him, as if I can actually touch Nico from way up here. He's running. "Nico ..." His name rips from my throat, my voice laden with desperation. "Seth ... we have to."

"We can't," Seth says as he holds me tighter.

My pleas erupt from the depths of my soul, a single, echoing plea that resonates across eternity— "Please." If Seth could just feel it, just understand.

Instead, his grip on me tightens like a vice, his determination to keep me from plummeting evident. But I can't tear my gaze away, and I can't leave him. I can't. "We have to go back. Stop, please."

Seth turns in the air, still holding me, so he can see Nico over my shoulder and I can't. We're still flying, being thrust by the force of his almighty wings, and I'm nothing but a ragdoll in his arms. His face is next to mine, his mouth so close, but I hear him in my head, his voice penetrating it. "We go back, we die."

As we roll back into position in the air, the wind steals my sob, and I hold onto Seth. Nico is a tiny figure standing against an enormous, menacing presence. It stalks him from the darkness, its fur bristling, gnarled claws glinting in the sunlight, and eyes aglow with otherworldly power. I don't even know what it is. *Run, oh, God, please run.*

My mind struggles to comprehend what is happening, and nothing seems to make sense. I feel Seth's chest pressing against mine as his magnificent wings propel us through the air at an astonishing speed, faster than I ever imagined possible.

We fly through the air like a bullet, the wind pushing past us, inviting us on our journey. Gravity no longer exerts its relentless grip on us; we're not plummeting as we did when Donovan threw me from the balcony and Seth caught me. Instead, we're... flying.

No. I'm wrong. We ARE falling.

The ground is coming too fast. We're nose-diving towards the canyon. My breath catches. "Seth—"

Before I can fully react, Seth's powerful arms encircle me, pulling me closer to his chest. He says the words that are like a song in my soul. "I've got you." Words he's whispered so many times before. I steal one last glance in Nico's direction, but he's long since vanished from my sight.

I close my eyes, burying my face in Seth's chest, placing my trust in him.

Trusting a vampire.

We fall.

CHAPTER
TWO

The creature charges relentlessly, hot on the heels of Seth and Payton. It tears across the lush green lawn, its claws slashing through the grass, propelling it faster

A guttural scream erupts from the depths of its being, morphing into a thunderous roar that reverberates through the daylight, a profound sound that envelops them all.

Even now, even after all this time, Seth wins.

But that won't last for long.

A seething hatred festers within the creature, and if hatred could translate into power, it would be the one in control.

With the creature occupied, Nico sees his chance—the only way out. He sprints, but not in the direction he and Payton came. That path is obstructed. The creature would spot him instantly. Instead, he dashes toward the fence, aiming to scale it and make a desperate break for freedom. It's a manoeuvre he's pulled off countless times with the Hallows, vanishing without a trace, vaulting over obstacles, and grasping a fleeting taste of liberty before his mother could find him.

Nico pumps his arms and legs, panic clawing at his soul. His breath is molten lava in his throat. Run, run, run....

Payton's voice echoes in the air, calling his name, guiding him with her urgency. Run.

Payton's father, Jonathan Summers, remains passive, a useless man. He watches in silence as Nico makes the grave mistake of looking over his shoulder, locking eyes with the relentless creature.

Hatred pours from it, thick and malevolent, a darkness that seems poised to devour anyone in its path. "No—"

But it's too late; Nico is spotted. The creature's strange eyes lock onto him. Nico inhales deeply, willing his body to push further, to extract every ounce of speed. The creature roars, rearing up.

"No.... Please—" Nico propels himself with determination, feet pounding the earth.

The creature closes in, running on all fours with thunderous power.

If only Nico could move faster....

The wall stands ahead—a daunting obstacle. But Nico has faced taller. He lunges toward it, reaching out with his hands, ready to grasp the top. His fingers make contact, and he struggles to pull himself up. But the creature is right behind him, lightning fast. Its massive paw swipes past Nico's back, a near miss that threatens to ensnare him.

Nico struggles with every ounce of strength left in him to hoist himself up, reaching desperately for that extra inch. A bead of sweat trickles down his temple, his heart pounding double-time in his chest. He taps into a well of energy he thought was depleted, his arms propelling him upwards with a grunt.

But the creature is faster. It catches him and yanks him down, its snarling face closing in on his. Its jaws snap with sharp, deadly teeth.

Nico's arms quiver as he clenches his teeth, a desperate battle for escape raging within him. He attempts to scramble away, but the creature drags him back with ease, a cat toying with its prey.

Fear squeezes Nico's heart like a vice, his attempts to scream producing only strangled cries. The creature's hot breath washes over his face, teeth bared, poised to strike.

"I'll rip you to fucking pieces." The creature's visage shifts, transforming into a man—Donovan. His transformation is grotesque, mid-change as his bones shift at an unnatural speed, faster than any shifter Nico has ever witnessed. The horrific sight forces the scream from Nico's throat, his stomach churning with dread.

The shift gives Nico a chance to escape. He takes it, but Donovan is an unstoppable force, closing in on him. Nico scrambles backward, frantically clawing at the ground in a desperate bid for escape. Donovan snags his ankle and jerks him backward, pulling him into a suffocating embrace.

Terror chokes Nico as Donovan's hand clamps around his throat. "Make a move, and I'll snap you in a second."

With effortless grace, Donovan rises, lifting Nico off the ground. Nico's only recourse is to grasp at Donovan's hand and wrist, trying to pry it away as he's hauled toward the door. Payton's father stands uselessly on the sprawling porch, a silent witness to the unfolding horror.

Donovan drags Nico inside and flings him toward two men—vampires.

"Take him downstairs."

The vampire on the left is dressed in a suit, his long dark hair pulled back, his bloodshot eyes not red like Seth's, but rather the crimson hue of a vampire on the brink of starvation, pushed to the very edge of thirst before being pulled back. A torturer for the undead.

Donovan's upper lip twitches as he strides across the hallway, where a woman holds out a robe for him. He slips it on, concealing his naked form. "Do not fucking touch him. He is mine. Take one bite, and I'll ensure you regret it for all eternity."

The man nods and bows. "Yes, sir."

Donovan exhales heavily, then turns to face Jonathan, who stands apart from the tumultuous scene. "I had her. I fucking had her. All you had to do was have her in here, and this would be done."

"I'm sorry...."

"Do not placate me with feeble human emotions. Next time, you will not fail."

CHAPTER

THREE

The ground is coming up so fast, too fast. I hold on to Seth and press closer into his body. He tightens his embrace, holding me closer.

His wings flap frantically, trying to keep us airborne, and he stays focused, ready to make an impact with the ground.

We hit and roll, me encased in the safe cocoon of his hold all over again, but I can't help but let out a gasp of shock at the suddenness of our fall. Seth grunts, but then stillness follows.

We lay there for what feels like eternity, my head on his chest and the sun beating down on us.

His heart is pounding in sync with mine, a deep bass thumping resonating through our bodies. "Seth ..." I whisper his name and it feels like we're one single being, connected in ways I don't understand.

I have to pull myself back, remember what he is and what he is to me.

His eyes and mouth are open, baring the tips of his fangs. The red circle around his pupils is bigger, as if he's just fed. Blood-red lines snake under his skin, a network of capillaries visible in the sun.

The sun ... My stomach does a somersault. "We have to get you inside—" I gasp, then stop abruptly. "Y-You're not burning."

He shakes his head slowly, his gaze so intense it feels like a physical force pushing against me. "No." The finality of that one word sends a chill down my spine.

But that is all he says.

I push myself off from him, and as soon as I am out of his hold, he sits up straight and his wings fold back in one graceful motion.

I feel so lost and strange. I'm not sure what I'm supposed to do. My body is warm from his touch, my nerves buzzing with the way the sun's rays beat down on us.

I want to ask Seth if he's okay. I want to ask him what I'm supposed to do, but years of training have my lips sewn shut.

He gets to his feet. His wings have folded back now, forming that intricate tattoo across his back. It's just as beautiful as they are, maybe more so. Shimmering blue waves under his skin, ready to come out when he needs them.

I don't move as I watch him take a step and stop in front of me. I hold still, ready for the anger, for whatever reprimand I'm due for leaving. I didn't mean to, but his kind won't care about that. Yet, inside, I don't feel the same level of fear. "Are you hurt?" is what he asks, taking me aback.

I shake my head.

The sun isn't burning his skin, and he can look straight at it. It doesn't make sense.

He turns and takes a few steps away from me. The

valley that used to be a river at the back of his building is now reduced to gravel and dirt that has dried in the relentless heat. Skin Trade stands out like a dark crystal shimmering in the bright light and reaching so high into the sky that I can't look the whole way up.

He ... we fell from there.

Skin Trade is built on the edge. Cracks in the ground create a webwork covering the dirt leading to his entrance. Small dark green plants dare to sprout out, but some leaves are so burnt, they're almost black. What is left of a few trees push out from the barren earth, forcing their life out of the riverbed.

"We should get inside."

I look back at his place. "We're going in there?" The words just tumble out and I grimace. I know I shouldn't question.

But he replies. "Yes. It will be dark soon, and what lurks in the darkness is worse than anything we might encounter in the daylight."

"Your brother—"

"If he has any sense about him, he'll not come here." He peers up at the tall building. Sweat glistens on his back as he takes another step, then stops. "Move back ..."

I don't know what he means, but I follow his lowered gaze. He's looking at the shadows, where the rocks create a dense overgrowth of bushes and trees. They lean together like they could fall at any second, but are being held up by their neighbours. A few spindly branches reach across our path and scratch along the ground, warding us off with their meagre strength. There are cars here, too—what was once an old kind of trailer looks familiar from my youth. My father used to have friends who had those kinds of campers.

Thoughts of my father play in my mind, and I don't even know how to sort through that part in all of this yet. The father in my mind and the one I just saw don't reconcile and I can't comprehend how they're the same person. In my mind, I envisioned him relieved, coming at me, finally putting his arms around me, glad for me to be alive, but instead ...

"Payton ..." Seth's voice is barely a whisper but I pick up the warning tone in it. He moves back to me and crouches. "Do not move."

He goes for the tree closest to us; it's charred and black at the top, like someone took a fire to it. And I know the sun has done that—the skies were scorched when the humans tried to fight back. Now it beats down unforgivingly.

Seth snaps off the branch and it comes away with a loud crack. Then I see what he is looking at and a gasp catches in my throat. "thirsty —" There are two, maybe three. The shadows near them move as if there are flames in the sunlight. No, there are four, five....

My breathing hitches.

They stalk the shadows, looking for an escape—some way to slip through to us. A female leads the way, her long blonde hair mottled with fiery red streaks. One of her ears holds a chain, and she still wears clothes—black and dark, like she died at a rock concert.

The man behind her is not so lucky. His face is burnt away. He has no eyes. His nose is gone, shrivelled to blackened shreds, and flakes flutter from his skin. He moves like a zombie, chewing on something that isn't there. His jaw moves rhythmically, gnawing on an invisible morsel. The others follow him closely, one missing both ears and half its skull, another with a single hole where its mouth should be, and yet another with chunks of flesh missing from his abdomen.

They're all staring at me, their fingers groping at the air for me as I stand before them. A meal waiting to be devoured.

My heart hammers relentlessly in my chest, a thunderous cacophony threatening to drown out all other sounds. I mirror Seth's actions, grabbing whatever branches I can from the burnt tree. The smaller branches crumble in my grasp as my fingers close around them, leaving my hands stained black.

"I've got this," he says.

If we didn't need to get into Skin Trade, we could have left these behind in the dark corner, simply walked away, and let them remain in the shadows. But they stand in our way now, blocking the path that leads us to the door, and to safety. I know if we had time to go elsewhere, Seth would take us. But there is no elsewhere, and the sun will set soon. Then they won't just be these few to contend with, but so many more. And whatever else lurks in the dark.

With predatory grace, Seth moves among them with fluid precision.

They pay him no heed, arms extended, gnashing teeth, seeming oblivious to his presence. Groans continue their relentless chatter and their outstretched fingers reach for me.

It's the decaying male nearest to me that inches the closest; little remains of his facial features, except one unseeing eye. The other is a bloody pit. His lips have peeled back from his teeth, exposing blackened gums and fangs.

His vacant gaze locks onto mine.

It mirrors the one I saw earlier when I was with Nico, the one whose former life I managed to glimpse like a shadow in my mind, or maybe a dream I made up. He steps boldly into the light, extending a trembling hand toward me. The sun beats down, the ever-patient weapon against these creatures poised to lay claim to the undead daring to traverse its path. The flesh that remains on his arms hisses in the heat, sizzling like cooked meat. A moment later, he glances at it, and for a fleeting moment, his disarrayed consciousness seems to register imminent death before his eyes widen once more and fixate on me.

He moves further into the sunlight, exposing more than just his hand. I step back towards Seth. It's like the one that followed me out from the Deathbringer's building, seeming to not care about their survival against the sunlight, focused only on reaching me. The sunlight strips away his flesh, and when it reaches his face, he doesn't flinch as it bubbles and oozes off his bones, a black tar running down his cheeks.

Inevitably, he collapses.

Seth stares at the pool on the ground, his brow furrowed. "It should not have done that," he says.

Before I can respond, he swings a branch around, striking the female. She hisses as she topples backward, her feet ensnared by the others already on the ground. They hiss at her, agitated by her rude intrusion as they try to scramble towards us. There is no coordination amongst them now; they've devolved into ravenous monsters craving only to feed their insatiable hunger, thanks to Alitoa—the virus humans had created.

Alitora had been a chance for humans to rid the world of vampires, only to have it backfire and create these creatures we see before us.

Seth swings for another, and then another. But these vampires—former vampires—are not vanquished so easily.

Seth wields a branch, driving it into their chests, then moving on to the next. The thirsty show no fear, and even as they tumble, they don't stop their relentless reaching. Seth struggles to hold them at bay.

With each blow of his branch, their undead forms splinter and fragment. The grotesque remains of their kind pile around him. He exhales heavily with each splintering body, yet they persist—a relentless force, determined to breach his defences and reach me.

"Seth—" I call out his name on instinct as one crashes into him, claws gouging his bare arm. Blood spills from the wound, but he keeps on fighting, trying to shake off its grip.

"Move—" he shouts, pushing me away while still striking at the creature. Helpless and useless, I watch in horror. Seth falls to his knees, rising again and again, even as the onslaught of creatures grows greater with each passing moment.

Amidst the chaos, a commotion emerges—a jarring blend of mechanical roars and aerial hisses, like a swarm of angry wasps growing to life somewhere beyond the bend of the riverbed.

But then I see them—Killian and Naneve, riding through the valley with swords in hand, slicing their way through the throng of thirsty creatures.

Bike rolling away behind him, Killian dismounts before it comes to a full stop. He raises his blade with practised ease, striking with precision to decapitate any creature that dares approach him or Naneve.

Breathless, desperate, I run toward them. "Seth, they—"

Killian nods, pushing me towards Naneve. She rides around us, slashing through the shadows. One severed head tumbles into the sunlight, dissolving as it hits, the body left at the side twitching.

Naneve and Killian race to Seth's side, killing all that get in their way.

"There are more over the hill," Killian says.

Seth gets to his feet and seems to physically shake himself. He casts a quick glance in the direction Killian and Naneve just came from. "How many?"

Killian wipes his sword on a rag from his pocket and tosses the rag to the ground. "Too many." Their gaze shifts from me to the riverbed behind me, stretching farther than my eyes can see.

"A herd," Seth states. "We need to get inside. We'll never hold them off." He takes a blade from Killian and tosses his branch aside, driving toward the remnants of a small group blocking our path. Without hesitation, he beheads them, chopping them down.

Blood and gore splatter in every direction. Between them, they clear the way, allowing Seth to pull out a panel from beside the door on top in a crouch.

"Inside," he directs me. I stand transfixed, a foolish paralysis rooting me in fear. Killian strides over to me, grabbing my arm to drag me inside.

Seth holds the door open for both of us and, once we're securely inside, locks it, sealing us off from the monsters.

I go to the door so I can watch them through the thick glass. They gather and move like liquid in the shadows. I feel the weight of their stare as they watch me. I can see the thirsty moving back, confused that they've lost me, unable to understand how I went into the door. But I feel so much more than that. I feel their hunger, their pain, their need, their suffering—it's thick, choking me inside.

One of the thirsty comes up to the glass and slaps a

hand against it. He peers in at me. His eyes are deep green, the colour of the ocean when you know there is danger beneath its surface. For a moment, he looks perfectly human ... but only for a moment. Then he opens his jaws and shows me his fangs.

Seth hunches over a desk, cradling his arm to his chest as he powers up a computer.

"I've never seen them move like this before," Killian says from beside me, his tone baffled. "We drove right through them to reach you and they ignored us both. They didn't even seem to acknowledge our presence. What the hell is happening?"

Small cannons, the same as are out front, push out from the ground and open shower-like heads. Seth clicks a series of keys and buttons, and the cannons fire out a red mist.

He nods at me, his gaze unwavering.

"They want her."

CHAPTER
FOUR

The red mist engulfs the thirsty, shrouding their senses in a bloodthirsty frenzy, deluding them into thinking they're feeding. It propels them into a frenetic dance, back and forth, luring them further into the unforgiving sunlight. For a moment, I watch them burn, one by one, and then it hits me. These are people—were people. Like the nurse, like the man. They had had lives and families.

Sometimes, dead is better.

I sink quickly into a nearby seat, averting my gaze from the windows. I can't bear to helplessly witness the thirsty's frenzied agony any longer—their faces contorted in silent screams, their lifeless eyes wide with horror. I've seen too much.

Turning away doesn't stop me feeling them, though. It tugs inside me like a hook, ripping at my insides with sharp claws. Their anguish is palpable, throbbing against my skin like a festering wound.

They want her.

Seth's words hang heavily in the air. I struggle to find a

response for what he said amidst the chaos that surrounds us. Everything unfolds in a whirlwind of speed and sluggish similarity.

Wrapping my arms around myself, I try to contain the jumbled mess inside my head. My thoughts are a chaotic storm.

Nico, the thirsty, the entire situation—it's all too overwhelming.

I never thought I'd be glad of the silence Crevan's place had offered me. At least there, I had had some semblance of order to my life, and some control. Everything was easier when I was told how to do it ... when to do it. But this ...

This is the price of freedom.

But then, am I really free? Are any of us?

The absence of structure leaves my mind spinning. I bow my head, allowing the turmoil to settle within me. In this moment, I feel utterly lost in the labyrinth of my thoughts, threatening to consume me entirely.

Seth, Naneve, and Killian talk as if I'm not present, and I seize the fleeting moment of invisibility to simply observe and quiet my restless mind.

The bunker, intended as a sanctuary, exudes opulence. It's a place constructed by someone with no concern for financial constraints, but a deep yearning for comfort. Even the part we currently occupy is spacious, its high ceilings creating an illusion of grandeur. The walls are adorned with polished marble surfaces, adding to the room's lavishness. Soft, ambient lighting bathes the space in a warm, welcoming glow, a stark contrast to the harsh world beyond.

Two separate rooms stand off to the side, offering both privacy and functionality. These rooms are furnished with equal opulence, boasting comfortable beds and luxurious furnishings. It's evident that no expense was spared in creating this haven.

Seth occupies the spacious, well-appointed bathroom, equipped with modern fixtures and amenities. The sleek counters, walk-in shower, and bathtub all contribute to the sense of luxuriousness. He stands by the massive sink, water running as he rinses his injured arm under the taps.

"Is that going to be a problem?" Naneve inquires.

"No," Seth replies, his voice steady. "It's just a flesh wound, and there was no infection from them. I'd feel it if there were."

I understand that pain, the searing sting when the Nostro slashed me on the shoulder. That heals slowly.

Naneve hops up onto a grand table nearby, leans back on her hands and starts swinging her legs back and forth. "So, what's the plan now? Are we staying here? Going back to Sanctuary?"

Sanctuary was the place they took Seth and me after we fell last time—a place where Donovan sent in a horde of thirsty.

Seth takes a deep breath, an act that seems strange given he's a vampire. "I need to clean this," he says, nodding down at his arm. "Then I'll feed, and after that, we'll assess what Donovan has left me beyond these walls."

He glances at the ceiling as if he can already discern what lies above.

My heart flutters at the thought of the people who once resided here. Who might be left? What devastation could Donovan have wrought? Nearly all of them were strangers to me, but they had lives, aspirations, and dreams. I clench my hands together tightly, not wanting to dwell on the possible horrors. This world has become so unbearably ugly.

Killian appears to share my concerns. "Do you think he has destroyed everything?" he asks while handing Seth a first aid kit. Seth accepts it, though his expression doesn't suggest he's thrilled about needing assistance.

The wound on Seth's arm still bleeds, and he grabs a towel to pat it dry. The white cotton comes away stained. "My brother has always been spoilt." He leans against the counter, one hand resting on the bloodied towel. His gaze meets mine in the mirror, crimson red-rimmed irises locking onto mine, sending my pulse racing. "He always destroys what he can't have." Then, just as swiftly, he looks away, redirecting his attention to Killian. "Give me an update on your people. What are the losses? And how did they miss Avery's treachery?"

Killian's demeanour shifts, visibly burdened by Seth's question. Guilt and shame weigh him down, and the mention of the 'Avery thing' clearly makes him uncomfortable. It's not just out of respect for Seth, but the shame he carries himself. "I don't have a clue. None of us saw it. I didn't even suspect. He was always so ... so damn ..." He sighs, lowering his voice, but the remorse is palpable. "I trusted him."

Seth maintains a stoic expression, his focus on Killian, devoid of anger. "Do not bear the weight of it. A mistake was made, but it cannot happen again."

"It won't happen again." Killian's conviction is unwavering, and even I find myself believing him. The determination in his words is absolute.

"Tell me about your men and women. I see Naneve survived her ordeal with Avery," Seth remarks, showing no hint of concern. I don't know what happened there, either. So much has changed after a decade in captivity, and all I know now is how to say yes and do as I'm told.

But it's Naneve who speaks. "That little prick got the drop on me. If he wasn't already dead, I'd do it myself."

"He fooled us all," Killian says before providing Seth with the requested information. "We lost many good fighters." He lists names I don't recognise, and my heart aches for them. No one should lose their life in this war. The suffering on both sides is gut-wrenching. "I left Sasha and Haily in charge. Dessie is okay, too. Tim is leading the group to secure the compound. The thirsty only breached the south wall. If he can't fix it before nightfall, they'll seal it off enough to protect it."

Naneve fiddles with her knife, holding it in one hand and turning it so it catches the light. "The thirsty shouldn't come back. If they smell the blood of their own dead."

"Then it'll repel them," Seth adds. "When the sun rises, get them moved. Talk to Austin. He should take them, at least the women and children. Donovan will know I'm not there, but he may strike just to anger me. When you followed me to the Summers' residence, there was a boy with Payton. Did you see him?"

"A boy?" Killian frowns. "The Hallows kid?"

"I saw him," Naneve confirms. "I was positioned on the tower at the old factory. Killian thought I wasn't ready to get into the thick of it."

"Avery had drugged you," Seth says.

Naneve dismisses the explanation with a shrug, but the anger in her eyes is unmistakable. "I saw him then. I was going to aim, but you came in and took Payton." She nods towards the crossbow resting with her belongings in the corner of the room, which she had taken off when they entered. She seems to have quite an arsenal.

Seth takes the kit Killian had given him and places it on a high table across the room. He lays his still-bleeding arm on the surface, three large gashes exposing the tissue and muscle beneath. He seems somewhat unnerved by it. "Does he live?" Opening the kit, he extracts a thread and needle, then lifts a questioning gaze to Naneve.

Even Naneve seems unusually off-kilter. Not that I know her well, but in the brief moments we've spoken, her words have always carried force. "Yes. Well ... they took him inside." Her gaze remains fixed solely on Seth as she speaks, determination in her eyes, but something else lingers there, something unspoken.

Seth's head tilts upward as he concentrates on the thread and his arm. It appears he's figuring out how to stitch his own wound with just one hand. When he raises his eyes to meet mine, he speaks, and there's a sense of relief in his words. "If they didn't slaughter him when we left, their intention is to keep him alive. If I know my brother, he would have taken him out unless he had a use for him."

I nod, pressing my lips together, feeling a tangible sense of relief. He's okay, and that knowledge lightens my heart somehow. I understand that he wouldn't have asked about Nico if not for me, and I'm grateful for that.

"Why do you think they want her?" Killian asks, moving around the table to assist him with the wound. Seth clenches his fist at his side, and the air around us grows tense. Accepting help clearly isn't something he's accustomed to. Seth's eyes flare red, and a tic works in his jaw, but he doesn't stop Killian from getting better access to the wound. We're all playing our parts here, pretending in one way or another.

"I have theories, but nothing concrete yet."

"You're thinking it has to do with her blood?" Naneve's voice carries a hint of scepticism.

"It's a possibility," Seth replies. "I've never witnessed the thirsty behave in such a manner as they did today. They came out of the shadows willingly, exposing themselves to the sunlight, all in pursuit of her. If I hadn't seen it with my own eyes, I might not have believed it. The thirsty may be deranged, but they understand the basic laws of self-preservation. What I witnessed out there ... they showed no regard for their own well-being."

I furrow my brow at Seth's explanation. "My blood?" I struggle to comprehend the gravity of that revelation, what it means, and the way Seth looks at me, the intensity in his eyes, leaves me with an unsettling feeling, as if he knows more than he's saying.

"It has to do with how you're able to walk in the sunlight," Killian says. "It has to do with all of this, you think?"

Seth focuses on his arm as Killian finishes stitching the wound. His expression remains serious. "I haven't walked in the sunlight in almost six hundred years."

I stare at Seth, my heart clenching in sorrow at his revelation.

Killian leaves Seth to finish cleaning his own wound, and retrieves a shirt from a nearby cabinet to hand him.

Seth slips the shirt on and his stare focuses on me. "Your blood runs through my veins." His voice is low and filled with intensity. He moves closer to me, and my heart skips a beat involuntarily. I don't resist as he takes my hands, pulling me up from the seat. His fingers are warm against my wrist, a stark contrast to the usual coldness of vampire hands. His touch sends shivers through my body. Softly, he runs a thumb across my healing wounds where his fangs had pierced my skin. "I feel you, too," he murmurs. "You call to me."

Gentle fingers lift my chin, tilting my head back. The moment his eyes meet mine, I'm falling, vanishing into some unfamiliar and inexplicable place. I can't look away. I can't move. He has me paralysed, consuming my entire soul.

I try to speak, but my mouth refuses to comply. "Seth ..." I manage to whisper, my voice catching in my throat. I have to close my eyes, allowing myself to succumb to every tingling sensation in my body.

Without warning, I'm plunged into a different time, a different place, and I can smell the earthy scent of grass and the comforting aroma of a wood burning in a stove. There's something cooking, too, a stew perhaps, and the scent of Seth surrounds me—a mixture of the outdoors, the lake, the mountains, all rolled into one intoxicating fragrance.

I can wrap myself in it, sink into it. I open my eyes to look around me, but Seth is right in front of me, our eyes still locked.

I stay silent, unable to articulate the questions burning in my mind. I want to ask him what just happened, what I experienced. I can feel my pulse pounding against his fingers, my breaths quickening.

But just as abruptly, he lets go and steps back, turning his attention back onto Killian and everything else at hand. "Grab whatever weapons you need. We're going into Skin Trade to see what devastation my brother has left in his wake."

CHAPTER
FIVE

I half-expect Seth to instruct me to wait, locking me in the room again, this time ensuring I can't escape. I brace for Naneve to shove me back, or for Killian to block my path.

Instead, Seth flips open a hidden hatch in the floor, revealing a handle. He tugs it, and a panel rises from the ground. My eyes widen at the sight—a cache of guns. Various shapes and sizes, they're arranged with the precision of art exhibits, waiting for admiration. But these are no mere exhibits; they're lethal, designed for precision killing.

I gasp, watching Seth. He's ready, not just for a battle, but for war, an assault on his fortress. This bunker, this sanctuary, serves more than just for healing and hiding; it's a war room, a command centre, ensuring readiness for battle.

Observing him, I wonder what war he anticipated. Such preparation hints at fear, but Seth radiates only strength and leadership.

Killian stands aside, not aiding Seth, yet I sense his urge to help. It's in his nature, just as it's in Seth's to lead alone.

"Do you need blood?" Naneve asks, rising from the table and joining Killian. They both eye the arsenal with evident hunger, Naneve's perhaps more intense. Were the weapons food, she'd be drooling.

"The effects of Avery's actions are fading," Seth dismisses Naneve's offer. "Nevertheless, there should be blood stored here if necessary, unless Donovan has destroyed it."

I remain where I am, unsure of my place amid these seasoned warriors and their familiar arsenal. In another life, another version of me, perhaps in a parallel universe, I'd know how to handle these. But for the last ten years, my experience has been limited to useless tools like butter knives, and I'm surprised we were even allowed to use those.

Then Seth, perhaps sensing my unease or simply understanding more than he lets on, grabs a small bag, and tosses it onto the table. He unfolds it, revealing knives with blades that gleam like silver. In the centre lies a belt. He examines it, then looks at me. "It might be a bit loose, but it'll work," he says, passing it to me. The moment our fingers brush, a jolt of awareness runs through me.

The belt, heavy and solid, somehow makes me feel connected to him, to this world.

Hastily, I secure the belt around my waist, pulling the leather strap tight enough to feel its burn against my skin. It hangs low on my slender hips, and I sense a weight of history, a tangible echo of despair from it.

"Choose your weapons." Seth gestures towards the array of knives he has arranged on the table. "You'll need to attach sheaths and hooks to the belt as well."

"You should take three blades," Killian advises. I frown

in confusion before he elaborates. "One for each hand and a spare on your back, in case you're disarmed."

My heart pounds, a mix of fear and adrenaline coursing through me. "Are you expecting a fight as soon as we step outside?"

Seth lifts his eyes to meet mine, and for a fleeting moment, I'm captivated. I see not just the vampire king, but something deeper, more ancient and familiar, resonating within him. It's as if he's calling to a part of me I hadn't known existed.

You call to me, he'd said.

Is it the same? Is it what I feel?

Seth's muscles ripple beneath his clothes as he prepares for what lies beyond. He makes me forget my past, my struggles. He inspires a sense of being more than I am, yet he does nothing overt to provoke this feeling within me.

Killian and Naneve arm themselves, while Seth is a weapon in his own right—no mortal could face a vampire and survive, and he is the Vampire King.

It takes Seth thirty minutes or so to get ready. Killian throws a questioning glance Seth's way when he flexes the fingers of his injured arm, but he doesn't voice the curiosity surely brewing within him.

I stand behind them, feeling like a mere shadow. My hands tremble as I dare to touch the hilt of my blade—it feels alive, almost pulsating in my grip. Despite its weight, it lends me a sense of strength.

"I do not know what we'll find in there," Seth says to Killian. The red in his eyes has infiltrated the whites, a web of intricate veins mirroring every emotion. "But whatever it is, my brother left it as a message."

His gaze meets mine again. In just a look, he conveys so much—understanding, reassurance, strength.

"If anything happens to me, ensure her safety." He's speaking to Killian, but I have no doubt Seth himself would do everything in his power to protect me. I feel it in my core, as real as my own heartbeat. I shouldn't have the right to that protection, yet when he looks at me, it's as if I am his world.

It knocks me off balance. I don't know what this is or what has changed.

He approaches the door, embodying his status and identity with self-assurance and pride. He carries himself as if everyone beyond that door is waiting for him, anticipating his arrival.

The door swings open, and we're immediately assaulted by the repugnant odour of death. "Oh, God," I mutter, covering my mouth to suppress the rising gag. The scene is vile, the air heavy with a malevolent presence. The stench—a grotesque blend of rotting flesh, stagnant moisture, and the sickly sweetness of broken dreams—clings to everything.

I take a deep breath, striving for composure. Contrary to my expectations, the place isn't shrouded in darkness but is bathed in harsh white light. The sun streams in unabated, revealing that someone has ripped down the shades meant to protect the vampires.

Seth's nose twitches, his senses keenly absorbing every detail around us.

With trembling legs, I step into the room, squinting through the thick, death-laden air. My heart pounds as I survey the horror enveloping us. The walls and ceiling are splattered with sticky dark red blood, the furniture reduced to unrecognisable heaps of twisted metal and wood.

On the ground, black char marks tell a grim tale—

vampires exposed to the sun, now reduced to mere ash and soot.

"He killed them," I whisper, more to myself than anyone else.

"Slaughtered them," Killian echoes grimly. "Sire?"

"We keep moving. There's nothing we can do for these now." Seth's words might be stark, but his expression reveals his true feelings—pain and anger.

Near the door to the main dance room, I see a pair of bare legs amidst a pool of blood. The body is twisted and torn, mangled beyond recognition. The woman's face is turned away, her back contorted unnaturally—a testament to brutal force. I don't need to see her face to identify her. The "C" branded on her hip says it all.

Maya.

The girl who'd escaped Crevan before me, the one who suffered so much at his hands, lies before us. I press my lips together, steadying myself and resisting the urge to rush to her. My heart hurts, both for her and for the echoes of my own past.

The silence is eerie. Through the large windows, I see dusk approaching, the sunlight turning a deep orange, signalling the day's end.

We move deeper into the bloodbath, past more bodies sprawled across the floor. Seth's expression remains stoic as he strides ahead, but there's a glint of vengeance and rage in his eyes. Each step echoes in the heavy air.

On reaching the lift, Seth halts at the sight of a man I remember seeing only a week ago. Seth kneels, touches the man's face with a gentle reverence, then slowly shakes his head in disbelief at the senseless carnage.

"He didn't do this alone," Naneve murmurs. "It looks like he came with an army."

Seth's jaw clenches as he surveys the devastation. "Knowing my brother, he did."

Our search through the floors is silent, introspective. We're presumably looking for survivors. Six floors up, and we've found no one. Despite the scattered bodies, the count seems less than the number of people present when this place was bustling. Maybe some escaped. Maybe many.

Emerging from the stairwell, I sense something. "Wait," I say abruptly, bringing everyone to a halt.

Naneve scowls, while Killian and Seth focus on me.

"Can't you feel it?" I ask, extending my hand. It's palpable, as if another person stands before me.

"You're sensing something," Killian rumbles.

My palms face forward, feeling the hair on my arms stand on end, attuned to an unseen force that doesn't seem to affect the others. It's like a vibration, a subtle but tangible energy coursing through me, unnervingly cold and unsettling.

But this strange sensation becomes inconsequential as a sudden, deafening crash resonates from one of the rooms along the hallway.

Seth reacts swiftly, Naneve hot on his heels. Killian hesitates for a brief moment, torn between confronting the unknown and his duty to protect me.

The layout resembles a hotel, rooms lined up side by side, and Seth cautiously approaches the third door along the hallway. As he pushes it open, the sound of sobbing reaches my ears.

"Tasha," Seth murmurs softly as he steps inside.

Tasha is hunched on the floor near the sofa, an overturned table beside her. The room mirrors the grotesque aftermath of what we witnessed in the main reception. A tempest of desperation has ravaged every corner, leaving behind a trail of utter chaos. Glass shards litter the floor, furniture lies in disarray, jagged claw marks scar the wooden surfaces, and the walls look battered and bruised, as if absorbing the anguish of the room's turmoil.

Tasha, the dancer from Seth's club, once full of confidence and finesse, is now a mere shadow of herself, her cocky demeanour replaced by an aura of vulnerability.

"Tasha, my darling....." Seth crouches beside her, gently tilting her chin to face him.

"I tried to help her—"

On the other side of the room, a large thick curtain catches Killian's attention. He pulls it back slightly. "Seth...."

"I didn't know what else to do. I tried ... I thought ..."

Seth motions Naneve overcome to Tasha's aid, then joins Killian by the window. As he opens the curtains, a sudden impact against the glass results in a gruesome splatter of blood.

A grotesque, contorted face appears on the other side, its features twisted into a nightmarish visage. The woman presses her face against the window, her fangs—one of which is chipped—visible as they scrape against the glass.

The horrifying reality dawns on me. "*Layla.*"

The vampire in Seth's employ had been thrown off the balcony by Donovan when she'd attempted to shield me, ultimately falling alongside Seth and me.

Now, I recognise the deranged gleam in her eyes, the same madness I had witnessed in the creatures that attacked us.

She's one of them now.

She is a thirsty.

CHAPTER SIX

Nico kneels on the hard floor, his knees aching with pain. It rumbles through him, urging him to stand and stretch to ease the discomfort. But he dares not move. The vampire looming before him is poised to strike, and any wrong move could cost Nico his life—a fact he's acutely aware of.

This vampire, the one who brought him down, radiates an unsettling hunger. His skin is pale, almost porcelain-like, and his eyes are dull, the vibrant red of feeding noticeably absent. The danger of an unfed vampire looms large; they're unpredictable, and even a slight movement could push this one over the edge.

Nico can tell he's being closely observed—the vampire's finger taps rhythmically to the beat of Nico's pulse. Then, with a flick of his tongue over his lips and a flash of fangs, the vampire looks down at him, triggering Nico's instinct to flee. In these moments, the ranting words of his stepmother Jackie, full of unrelenting hatred for their kind, echo in his mind. He's tempted to agree with her.

Another vampire stands guard by the door. He's pale,

too, but unlike the first, he has recently fed, though his lingering hunger is palpable. One word from him, and Nico knows they would tear him apart in a savage frenzy, fighting over flesh and blood. His life could end in less than sixty seconds.

Nico rubs his hand slowly down his thigh, an attempt to alleviate some of the ache. Fear and a flicker of relief battle within him at the sound of heels clicking on the cold, hard floor outside. They're approaching. He inhales deeply, and the vampire emits a low growl.

Stay still. Stay utterly still.

He doesn't lift his gaze as the door opens and the owner of the deep red heels enters. He catches only a glimpse of delicate feet, smooth skin, and perfectly sculpted legs. Moments later, they're joined by larger, black, sleek shoes—those of a man.

The sight tightens Nico's muscles.

Please don't. Please don't.

Before he can react, he's yanked to his feet by large hands. One hand wraps around his throat, lifting him until only the tips of his toes scrape the ground. Donovan Hayden's face hovers inches from his own. "We're going to talk, you and I. When I ask you a question, you're going to answer me. Do you understand?"

Nico's hands claw at his throat, desperately trying to ease Donovan's vice-like grip, but his efforts only seem to make Donovan tighten his hold more. Donovan's thumb digs into the edge of Nico's jaw so forcefully, he fears it might dislocate.

"Yes," he croaks.

"Then we should get along just fine." Effortlessly, Donovan flings Nico into a chair that seemed to have appeared out of nowhere. He hadn't even noticed them moving it, nor the vampire who now stands behind it. Nico lands hard, his back striking the chair, and hands immediately clamp down on his shoulders, pinning him in place. "Try to move, and we end you."

But it's the owner of the red shoes who steps forward. Nico has never seen her before, yet he instantly knows her identity: Amelia. Her reputation is infamous.

She is the epitome of beauty, untouchable and ethereal. Her perfection is almost sculptural, as if chiselled by divine hands. Her lips, a vivid red matching her shoes, part to reveal her fangs. But despite her beauty, Nico senses her age, a trait most humans can detect in older vampires.

Johan, his mother's lap dog and second in command in the Hallows, would often say, "We can detect the death in them. That's why they must all be killed."

Nico remembers how Johan and his stepmother, Jackie, mercilessly executed a vampire who was scarcely older than a teenager in her human years, justifying it as a punishment for an imagined debt. That moment was a turning point for Nico, when he began to see that some vampires retained their humanity and wished to cause no harm.

Amelia leans in, the nail of one long finger trailing along Nico's jawline. She observes him closely, her sinister smile hinting at pain and suffering. "He's so young. A baby," she purrs, but her tone is devoid of sympathy. "I bet he tastes really good. Sweet." Her face moves closer to his, her lips nearly touching his skin. Nico fights the urge to swallow, to show any fear, but inside, his pulse races, betraying his terror to Amelia, who laughs in response.

This was definitely Amelia, a name whispered among humans along with three others: Donovan, Marcus, and their King, Seth Hayden—each feared for their own reasons.

"You might find out soon enough." Donovan pushes the sleeves of his white shirt up, revealing strong, toned arms. His body is a testament to strength and definition, muscles evident even through the fabric of his black trousers. An intricate tattoo adorns one arm, drawing the eye with its detail. "Tell me about Payton Summers."

Nico's gaze shifts from Amelia to Donovan, even as Amelia trails her hand along Nico's chest, her murmurs about his soft skin and warm pulse a haunting undercurrent. When she stands With catlike movements, she moves to stand behind him, then slices open his t-shirt with a nail and slips a frigid hand inside the torn fabric.

Nico tries not to react to the chilling touch.

"I don't know her. I—"

Donovan raises an eyebrow. "She was with you just a few hours ago."

"I mean, I don't know much about her. We just met," Nico clarifies, struggling to maintain composure under Amelia's unsettling caress. "I know who she is, but that's all."

Donovan seems to accept this explanation. "How did you meet?"

"On the street. She was walking in the daylight, and it was hot. I offered her some water."

"And she took it?"

"Yes."

The room falls silent for a moment, Amelia's hands now both at the tear in his shirt. "You smell so divine," she whispers. Nico shudders.

"Explain everything to me," Donovan commands. "From meeting her to today. Every detail."

Nico frowns, recalling the events. They feel distant yet are so recent. "I was out looking for antibiotics," he starts. The scarcity of medicine is a constant struggle, something Donovan clearly has no interest in. So Nico shifts to the encounter with the thirsty. "They were in the buildings around us, trying to reach her. I pulled her into the road so we could walk, and then—"

"The thirsty were reaching out in daylight?" Donovan interrupts, his tone sharp.

Nico blinks, surprised. "Yes."

"And they were reaching for her specifically? Or just reaching out in general?" Donovan inquires, his voice edged with curiosity.

Nico recalls the scene vividly—the way the creatures extended their arms, their desperate attempts to grab her. The Nostro, a terrifying hybrid in the vampire world, were involved, too. "Reaching," he confirms.

Nostro, vampires infected with the virus that created the thirsty but who had also infused themselves with lycanthropy in a desperate attempt to combat it. The result was monstrous: starved, nearly deranged beings with the ability to think, plan, and calculate.

"For her." Donovan turns away, rubbing his well-defined jaw in thought. "Continue."

Nico stares at Donovan's back, a rising sense of dread and guilt forming a knot in his stomach. He's betraying her, a thought that haunts him, though he can't fathom why.

When Nico remains silent, Amelia's nails dig into his flesh, eliciting a quiet whimper of pain. Her grip is deceptively strong.

"We got chased," Nico finally says.

"The thirsty chased you in daylight?" Donovan asks.

"No, the Nostro. It emerged from a building and

pursued us. It cornered us near the old factory and delivery line." The image of the Nostro, grotesque and stuck mid-transformation, looms in his memory. "It didn't behave normally. It was ... trying to act human."

Donovan turns to face him with a frown. "Act human?" Nostros were known for their wild, animalistic behaviour. "Explain."

Nico swallows hard. "It was speaking," he says shakily. "Trying to communicate, but it was distorted, slurring between growls and speech. As if fighting an internal battle."

Amelia's grip on Nico's shirt relaxes slightly, allowing him to breathe more freely. "Then she did something...." He struggles to make sense of the memory. "There was a loud pop, my ears rang, and the Nostro screamed."

"You mean like a human?" Donovan asks, his expression inscrutable.

"Yes ... no ... maybe. It was a mix, a scream intermingled with growls. Then it fled, and so did we ... in the opposite direction."

Donovan's face gives nothing away, but Nico can see him processing the information. "And after that? You didn't encounter the Nostro again?"

"Yes," Nico says, nodding. "It returned, not alone this time. Two more Nostro were with it."

"They do not usually collaborate. What do you mean? Like a team? Like in a fight?"

"A team. We ran. That's when my mother ... when Jackie ..." He hesitates, the word 'helped' not quite fitting. She had taken them, scolded, threatened, and locked Payton up. But none of that seems to matter to Donovan, who neither asks for details nor probes further.

"And did you see them again after that?"

"No. We were in the safe house. It's impenetrable."

Something flickers across Donovan's expression, perhaps a hint of a challenge to Nico's claim, but he lets it pass. "What did Payton say when she touched the Nostro and it fled?"

"Nothing. She didn't understand what it was."

Donovan's questions oscillate between the Nostro and the thirsty, pressing Nico to clarify the events repeatedly. He speaks of leaving the Hallows but omits details about their escape. Donovan may instil fear in his body, but Jackie terrorises his very soul.

Donovan's gaze turns distant, reflective. Amelia watches him, her expression darkening. "Is she awakening to her powers?" Her voice is a blend of curiosity and unease. "Her touch caused the Nostro to flee. That's beyond human."

"It's possible," Donovan muses. "Her reaction to the Nostro … it suggests something dormant within her is awakening."

Amelia tilts her head, considering his words. "But does she even know what she can do? It seems like she's unaware of her potential."

Donovan cocks his head to the side. "That's the intriguing part. If she is oblivious to her abilities, she's a wild card. Unpredictable. It could be an advantage or a complication for us."

Amelia purses her lips. "An untrained power is like a loose cannon. If she truly has magic, understanding it and controlling it would be vital. Especially if she's just discovering it."

Donovan pins Amelia with a stare. "We need her here. If her powers are emerging, she could be more valuable than we anticipated. Or more dangerous."

Amelia smirks, a glint of excitement in her eyes. "Either way, it seems we have more than just a simple human on our hands."

"Oh, she's always been more than a simple human." His attention turns back to Nico. "Do you know where Seth has taken her?"

"N-No." And if he did, would he tell them?

Donovan's eyes narrow, suspicion evident. "You're lying, Nico."

Nico attempts to shake his head, hindered by Amelia's unyielding grip. "I-I swear, I-I don't know."

Donovan grabs Nico's collar, yanking him forward. "Do. Not. Lie. You know where they are, and you *will* tell me."

Panic surges in Nico's chest.

Amelia leans closer, her whisper for Donovan's ears. "You can leave him to me. I'll extract the truth."

Nico's heart races with dread. "I-I s-swear, I-I d-don't know...."

Donovan's grip tightens painfully, and his eyes darken, the red swirling ominously. "You know, Nico. *Tell* me. Where are they?"

Amelia's nails suddenly press deeper, drawing blood. "Speak, Nico," she drawls, her gaze malicious.

Nico clenches his teeth against the pain. "I-I don't k-know," he gasps. The fear is suffocating.

Donovan rises back to his full height and tuts. "That's very disappointing, Nico." He gives Amelia a nod. "Keep him alive. He'll be useful." He smirks. "A valuable bargaining chip."

CHAPTER
SEVEN

Seth's eyes seem to bleed, like ink spreading around the whites of his eyes. Layla, once a delicate beauty, is now a grotesque caricature of herself. Her skin is pallid and ashen, her hair a wild tangle resembling a bird's nest. Layla is replaced by a gnashing zombie-like visage.

As I watch her, it feels as if my heart ceases to beat, breaking into countless shattered pieces. Although I hadn't known Layla for long, I can read people. I distinguish the good from the bad, the intentions to harm from those of kindness. I had sensed her nature; she had always been nothing but kind to me. She didn't deserve this fate.

"Is this because of her fall?" I ask, my voice barely above a whisper. None of us move, each paralysed by the sight before us. Tasha remains on the floor, her knees pulled up to her chin, her arms wrapped tightly around them as she trembles. Her eyes are deep, dark voids.

Seth stares at Layla, and I can almost feel the waves of sadness emanating from him. She had been with him for so long, and though the duration remains uncertain, her loyalty and love for him were unmistakable. I expect, in his own way, he love her in return.

"If she had no blood to heal herself," Seth begins, finally tearing his gaze away from her to address me, "then her body will have consumed what's already within, entering a state of starvation." There is a gentleness in his eyes, a stark contrast to his inherent authority. It's a skill honed over centuries of existence, blending strength with compassion.

Practice, I assume. When you're as ancient as he is, such complexities become second nature.

Seth's focus returns to Tasha. "Tasha, my darling, how long has she been here?"

"Three days," she replies, her voice trembling with the weight of her words. "Three. I found her—" her sentence is interrupted by a sob, although no tears accompany it. Perhaps she has none left to shed, having given all of herself to sorrow. I've been in that place before, where the tears just run dry. I've cried so intensely it felt like I had nothing left to give. She places a hand over her mouth, and through our differences, my heart breaks for her. "Donovan came down and said you were dead. He said you'd fallen and that you'd died. I ..." She shakes her head, pulls her legs up to herself, and cries for a moment.

When she lifts her head, her eyes are red around the rims, her face puffy.

Seth maintains his silence, understanding there are moments when words need not be spoken, when the unspoken truths loom heavily in the air. He grants her the gift of silence, recognising her pain.

"I found her in the shadows." Her words tumble over each other in a desperate attempt to convey the urgency of the situation. Panic creeps into her voice, causing her speech to become rapid and clipped. "Those thirsty, those fucking—They were circling her like fucking vultures. They were waiting for her to die. Just waiting. Like they'd feed the moment her eyes closed and I ... Fucking pieces of shit." She wipes her eyes, her trembling hands revealing the depths of her distress. "I got her inside, and I—we ... I put her in your private box. I know you use it for ... for ..." The sob takes her. "I didn't know what else to do."

Killian steps in front of the door we just came through, standing protectively. Naneve moves closer to Tasha, but her gaze is locked into the box, her blade in her hand. I move to go more into the room. Not sure where I'm supposed to stand, but by the door with Killian doesn't seem right.

Seth puts his hand up. "Stop," he says to me.

I freeze mid-step. A game of musical statues when the disc jockey turns the music off.

"Go back to the door."

I frown but do what he says.

The room is silent as I walk through it. It's not a large room, similar to the one I stayed in when Seth first brought me here. A spacious hotel room—executive suites. I'm not sure why these thoughts occupy my mind. Perhaps it's deflection.

"Now stop. Walk back to Tasha," Seth instructs calmly and evenly. "Walk slowly."

Tasha's gaze flits between me and Seth. Her face is pale—I notice that now. Dark streaks mar her cheeks, and her lips are chapped. I wonder how long she's been holed up in this place with a crazed vampire. Brave, or maybe a little foolish? If Layla had escaped, Tasha wouldn't have stood a chance.

I walk slowly, glancing between Seth and Killian, hoping for answers, but even Killian is frowning.

"Stop and walk to Naneve."

I want to ask him why, but I comply, even if it feels foolish.

Naneve's eyes widen with uncertainty as we watch Layla frantically claw at the glass walls of her box. "She's following her."

Layla presses her fingers into one of the tiny vents along the side, trying to pry it open. Her white teeth are bared in an animalistic snarl, and her gaze burns through me.

Seth steps forward and opens a panel on the side of the glass. "Layla, my love," he says, softly.

She spares him only a glance before turning back to snarl at me.

"She understands," I mutter, taking a step towards Tasha.

Seth nods. "Yes. Killian, go to the next level—room 209—and bring back the male."

"The room with the couple?"

Seth nods again. "Yes. He should still be warm. I don't think he's been dead too long. Bring him up."

When we searched the place, each room, like 209, told tales of tragedy and death, silent witnesses to the grim reality of what Seth's brother was capable of. The rooms, once vibrant with energy, now echo with a haunting stillness.

Each room tells the same story—an abrupt end to life. Some harbour couples, frozen in their final embrace, while others contain solitary figures, their lonely demise speaking volumes of their last moments.

As we moved through the place, the presence of death was overwhelming, lingering thick and oppressive in the air. I don't envy Killian having to return to that. Donovan has caused so much death.

I furrow my brow, a knot of worry forming in my stomach. "Won't that kill her?" My eyes shift to Layla, her frenzied state still etched in my memory.

Seth's gaze remains fixed on her, his expression pensive. "No," he replies. "It should calm her."

I can't help but wonder about Layla's fate as I watch her desperate attempts to break through the glass.

"Do you think she can come back from this?" Naneve asks.

"Perhaps. Her eyes aren't completely glazed over yet. Maybe true death hasn't entirely taken her, leaving only basic instincts to animate her body. We will try this, and if it doesn't work, then I will end her."

CHAPTER
EIGHT

It doesn't take Killian long to return with the body. He carries the lifeless male over his shoulder like a discarded ragdoll as he pushes the door open and steps back in. The couple must have perished in the midst of passion and feeding. The man is dressed in nothing but cuffs around his wrists and a collar at his neck, pretending to be a blood slave. Little did they know the harsh reality of it.

His back is smeared with blood and a dark, glistening bruise. He's been stabbed, perhaps with stakes, but he isn't a vampire. He's human—a man who worked for Seth—and a vampire who paid for his services.

"Payton, please go and stand next to Naneve," Seth instructs.

I comply, keeping my gaze locked on Layla the entire time. She scratches frantically inside the glass box, trying to reach me. Her claws scrape against the glass, her mouth opening and closing as if trying to speak. A pang of guilt wells up inside me.

I'm sorry, Layla.

I never meant for any of this to happen. I was so naive and fell for Donovan's tricks, plunging us all into this situation. If I could just go back and change it ... I hope one day I can tell her and explain what happened. I hope one day I can ask her to forgive me. Maybe I can ask them all.

I draw in a shuddering breath. Layla's cognition has deteriorated so much, she doesn't seem to understand Seth is using me to distract her while he opens the door. I do, though, and it creates a tightness in my chest, and an urge to watch him, to warn him because I can feel her hunger. It pools inside me.

She's so focused, she doesn't even react when he taps the panel to release the lock. He steps inside. That does get her attention, though her reaction is limited to a low, resentful snarl over her shoulder. Seth nods to Killian through the glass for him to bring in the male.

Without turning his back on Layla, Seth accepts the body, cradling it in his arms. The man's head lolls back, his arm dangling limply at his side. His eyes remain open, his mouth agape. I wonder if it's a look of shock frozen on his face or the ecstasy from having fed a vampire. Feeding a vampire creates pleasure, orgasms, and sensations that we've never experienced before. It's why some humans become addicted to them. There's also the adrenaline-fuelled euphoria they can invoke. Humans are slaves in every sense to their whims, and Seth is the strangest master I've ever served. He has many, yet takes very little.

"Layla," Seth coaxes. "Little darling, come here."

Her snarling intensifies, and she scrunches her nose, resisting the urge to obey. "Layla ..." His voice takes on a mesmerising quality that all vampires possess. It's not just the words they say, but the vibrations in the air, the way they manipulate our brains. It's like a song they sing, a lullaby. Seth is the pied piper, and Layla is the mouse. But she's putting up a fight, desperately scraping at the glass and focusing on me.

Seth places the body in the centre of the room, rolling it onto its front. He doesn't move away but remains crouched, his eyes locked on her. I've been around vampires long enough to recognise when they're controlling humans or other vampires. Vampires can't fully control each other, except for masters and their creations. But Seth is a King, and maybe that affords him more power over others than any typical vampire.

Layla ceases her desperate attempts to break through the glass and lowers herself to the floor.

She lunges at the corpse in a frenzy of predatory hunger, her features distorting into a ravenous visage. She doesn't waste a moment before sinking her teeth into it. Her eyes become feral orbs, blazing with insatiable hunger. A river of red runs down her chin as she feasts, staining her pallid skin.

Seth takes a step back, still within the confines of the box, but he watches her as she bares elongated, sharpened fangs that tear into the lifeless flesh with savage determination.

I avert my gaze. It feels cowardly, as if I'm avoiding confronting something I should face, but I can't help it. If I could, I'd cover my ears, escape to another room, and not bear witness to this macabre feeding. I know the man is already dead, and it shouldn't matter, but it does. He had a life, a family, and so much more.

I try to look as Seth calls Layla's name again, his voice gentle yet controlling. Layla has calmed now, her face smeared in blood, her lips glisten with it. Seth's soothing voice seems to be having an effect.

"Layla, come to me," he says once more.

With only a slight hesitation, she goes to his arms, fully under his control.

Her transformation from frenzied monster to a subdued figure in Seth's arms is striking. Her eyes, once wild with hunger, now seem distant and unfocused. I guess that's good.

She's like a baby after a hearty feeding, her gaze almost rolling back into her head. My mind inexplicably recalls what my mother used to call a "milk coma." It's a strange association, but it somehow fits this surreal moment.

In Seth's hold, Layla resembles a life-sized doll, a floppy, compliant creation. He gently wipes the blood from her face and brushes back her dishevelled hair. His whispered words to her are too soft and quiet for me to discern.

Moving with the grace of a practised caregiver, Seth transports Layla to a nearby bed inside the box. He positions her between his legs, her back nestled against his chest. One of his arms encircles her protectively, holding her close. Her head rests against his shoulder, her eyes and mouth partially open.

With deliberate care, Seth extends his wrist and sinks his teeth into his own skin. Blood begins to ooze out, forming ruby red droplets. He positions his wrist over her mouth, waiting patiently. She stirs, clearly fatigued from her feeding, but gradually, she raises her hands and gently holds his wrist in place.

This time, her actions are tender and delicate. She's learned to savour the substance provided. Maybe that means there is hope, that he can bring her back. She suckles at his wrist with a gentleness that contrasts starkly with her earlier feeding.

The room is silent, save for her suckling sounds, as we

all watch with a mix of concern and anticipation. Naneve is ready with her blade.

Killian moves around the room, and I'm not entirely sure what he's doing. But none of us pay him much attention, not even Tasha. We're all engrossed in watching, which is why when he speaks, it makes me jump.

He has the curtains to the balcony open, and one of the doors, too. He's peering outside. "Sire," he says, addressing Seth with his usual formality.

Seth's own fangs are fully extended now, piercing his lower lip, and his eyes seem to glow, but he meets Killian's gaze. "What is it?"

Killian peers at him over his shoulder. "We have company."

CHAPTER NINE

Seth bursts through the glass, and in an instant, he's standing shoulder to shoulder with Killian. Killian, undeniably a formidable male, pales slightly in comparison to Seth's towering frame. Seth stands at least two inches taller, and while both are impressively built, Seth seems decisively more imposing and stronger. Perhaps this is an integral aspect of his identity, an essential element of the vampire mythos.

Both men's gazes fix on a horrifying scene unfolding before them. Seth's grip on the railing tightens, his knuckles whitening with the strain.

"What's happening?" Nanave has to crane her neck to peer around both men, who dominate the space. She freezes as she catches sight of the chaos, the silence in the room becoming charged. "Oh hell no. What the heck is that?"

"Did Donovan do it again?" Killian asks, likely referring to Donovan's issue of letting them in to decimate the army of Seth's Death Bringers.

I spot a small curtain off to the side, near a small table.

Rushing over, I yank it back, revealing a window that offers a view of the outside world—or more precisely, the area within the confines of the Skin Trade. Seth has created a bewildering illusion: a towering structure with rooms and balconies, all beneath an exterior façade, yet it is meticulously controlled. A canopy shields everyone from the sun's scorching rays during the day and retains warmth during the bone-chilling nights.

Emergency exit lights illuminate the area below, designed for the humans' needs. Vampires, of course, have no use for such artificial light; they thrive in darkness.

From my limited vantage point, I can see the foyer. It's not the darkness that stirs emotion, but the ravenous army below. These vampires, deprived of proper blood for so long, have lost almost all semblance of sanity. They've pried the door open, shattering one side of the glass. Their wretched forms are grotesquely disfigured, some missing patches of skin, with only remnants of clothing clinging to them. Their hair, if they have any, is matted and filthy.

They snarl and scramble over one another, their combined force pressing against the door's sheer pane of glass. It shivers and shatters into a cascade of shards, but they seem oblivious to the danger. If anything, it spurs their frenzy, driving them onward, faster, as the opening widens.

Survival drives them, a desperate need to feed, yet it's a futile endeavour. Now they seem beyond reason, propelled solely by primal instincts. My knowledge about them is limited, gleaned only from what I've heard from others.

As they swarm, their sights lock onto the lifeless bodies scattered across the floor. One after another, they join in the gruesome feast, converging like a pack of deranged vultures. Their inhuman snarls and screeches fill the air, a cacophony of sounds that's nothing short of nightmarish.

It's an unending wail that pierces through my senses. I want to cover my ears, to block it out, but I know it would be a futile gesture. It's the kind of sound that echoes in your mind, growing louder with each horrific moment.

Eventually, they focus on a single body, forming a monstrous circle, tearing at its flesh with the ferocity of wild animals. They are no longer sentient beings but ravenous beasts.

"The thirsty," I utter in a trembling whisper.

Seth leans over, observing the thirsty below, who remain oblivious to our presence. "The systems outside must be shut off," he muses, likely referring to the cannons outside, the same ones activated in the bunker. I remember them vividly from my first night here when Seth brought me after purchasing me. Like out back the cannons rose from the ground, emitting a bright red mist, deceiving the thirsty into thinking they were covered in blood, likely laced with some toxin. There were guards stationed outside, poised to fire at any of the creatures that drew near. "They might not be the most intelligent creatures, but it won't take them long to figure out how to reach the higher floors," Seth notes.

"They are occupied for now," Killian says.

"Aye, but not for long." Seth turns and approaches me. It's not that he's coming specifically to me, but rather into the room. I catch the moment he steadies himself against the door frame. If it were possible for a vampire to lose colour from their face, Seth does just that. I'm about to ask if he's alright, but he seems to anticipate my concern. He looks directly at me and subtly shakes his head, a gesture so slight I almost miss it. But I understand and remain silent, asking nothing.

. . .

He inhales deeply, his chest expanding as he attempts to regain his composure. If Killian and Naneve notice his momentary falter, they make no comment.

Once he's back in control, Seth strides over to the glass box and the control panel, inputting a sequence. A hissing mechanism activates, and a red light blinks in the corner, indicating action. He nods toward Layla. "You should be safe in there as long as they don't breach the glass. But it won't be easy for them. I need to head to the base level, to the office. The control panel for the cylinders is there. We need to get them firing before the horde figures out how to get up here." He meets Killian's gaze squarely. "King or not, I fear their sheer number might even be too much for me."

Killian closes the balcony window, muffling the disturbing sounds from below. "It's on the ground floor?" he asks.

"Aye, where else would it be?" Seth's response isn't directed at Killian with sarcasm but rather at the situation itself. "We can reach it if we make it to my room. We'll take the private lift. Though I suspect the power will be out, and we'll have to use the stairs. The problem is, however, the stairs and lift lead directly into the middle of that mess," he says, gesturing towards the balcony.

I can still see them through the small window. A swarm of bodies scavenging for every morsel they can find. How long before they clear it all and come searching for more? "Is there some kind of poison in the red mist?"

"Vampire blood," Killian reveals.

"But will it kill them?"

Seth nods. "Aye; the thirsty cannot survive on that which is undead. They require life or recently living blood."

Naneve frowns. "How do we get through them? If the control panel is in the lower room, how do we reach it?

They'll swarm us the moment we step out of the stairwell. And like you said, there are too many of them."

"WE NEED A DISTRACTION," I say, my voice a mere whisper, uncertain but determined. It's the only strategy I can think of to divert them away. If they step out now, the swarm below will engulf them, and as Seth has admitted, their numbers are overwhelming.

I half expect Naneve to dismiss my suggestion with a scoff, but she doesn't. "What kind of distraction? You mean yourself?"

Killian turns to me, realisation dawning. "They're drawn to her. Even the one that got in here went after her." He understands what I'm implying.

"I will not put you in their path," Seth growls, his protectiveness evident. "They will kill you, and it will all be for nothing."

"And if they kill you, where does that leave us?" I blurt out, then immediately regret my brashness. I bite my tongue, wishing I could retract my words, but Seth doesn't scold me.

"I will not risk anyone. We will get down to them and deal with it ourselves," Seth insists.

"But she's right," Naneve says. "If you die ..."

Seth ignores her. "We'll take the stairs, not the lift. If it's working, they'll hear it. We'll arm ourselves with blades and stand together. We can cut them down and push through. The door to the control room is less than six feet from the stair door. We can make it. Once inside, they can't reach us. We'll deal with them, then figure out the rest."

He approaches me, and for a moment, I see the man, not the vampire. Something inside me wants to reassure him, to tell him we'll find a way. It's almost as if I've said these words to him before, the echoes ringing in my mind.

But this is not the moment for such assurances.

I wish I could reach out and touch his face, but it's not the face of the vampire I see. Instead, we're somewhere else entirely, in a cabin with flickering firelight casting shadows around us. I wish he'd stop projecting these images into my mind. I don't understand their purpose, but as I come back to reality, I see him watching me, his expression unreadable.

"I don't want to stay here," Tasha interrupts, her voice cutting through the tense atmosphere. She tries to rise, her hand bracing against the seat. Her demeanour is less shaken than before, but far from composed. "Please ... don't leave us here."

Seth doesn't approach her. He shakes his head. "It's safer for you to remain here. There's less risk if you and Payton are secured in this place."

"What if they get up here?" Tasha's voice trembles.

"They won't. We're too high up, and they have to navigate the stairs. It'll take them time, and by then—"

"They'll be nothing but ashes," Killian finishes for him.

Seth's gaze returns to me. "Lock the door when we're gone. Under no circumstances should you open it, and don't even think about leaving this room." The last part is a clear reference to my previous wandering, an inexplicable decision that landed us here.

"Okay," is all I manage to say.

Seth's gaze lingers for a moment, and there it is again, that unsteadiness in him. Something feels off, a subtle imbalance, but I can't tell if it's real or just my own unease reflecting back. He staggers slightly, then steadies himself, holding the door frame a moment too long before stepping out.

I close my eyes, silently pleading for their safe return.

The door shuts behind them, leaving Tasha, Layla, and me in the room. Layla lies still where Seth left her, but I know she isn't dead. I can sense it, feel the alteration in her very essence. I press my palm against the glass, watching her, but she remains motionless.

"This is your fault, you know?" Tasha's words slice through the silence, bitter and resentful. "If you hadn't come here, if Seth hadn't bought you ..."

I stay silent, her words not frightening me. I've endured worse during my time with Craven. Sometimes, the women were more terrifying than the vampires, especially when I was just starting out in that world. It was a brutal hierarchy, and as I climbed through the ranks, more due to age than effort, I never became one to inflict pain on those newer and younger. The world is terrifying enough without making it worse.

Instead of responding, I move away from the glass box and approach the balcony to look outside more deliberately. I need to see if Killian and Seth are okay.

Below, at least three dozen of the thirsty are piling up, creating a grotesque spectacle. It's chaotic, devoid of any order, like a bizarre, frenzied congregation. It reminds me of the concerts my mother used to attend, with crowds cheering in theatres. But this is different, an unnerving display of desperation as they all head in the same direction.

OUTSIDE, beyond the expensive panes of glass, the darkness moves like liquid. I catch glimpses of blinking lights from other buildings, the city beyond the doors Seth drove me through. Businesses, the outside world. It's clear why the thirsty have congregated here; this place might offer food without the threat of immediate death.

One of them, a man who might have been old in his former life, turns towards me. Grey hair adorns his head, but a bald patch is prominent at the centre. His face is battered, bloodied. He doesn't strike me as a longtime thirsty, not with the determination etched into his features. His lifeless eyes betray his true nature, as do his hands clawing at the air.

He raises a hand towards me, his mouth opening. I'm certain he's trying to speak, but his words are lost to the distance, his mouth moving silently.

Beside him, a younger man, perhaps of Asian descent, also turns to gaze at me. Our eyes meet. The graininess in his eyes is deep, pronounced. His face, more decayed than the older man's, suggests he's been a thirsty for longer, despite his youthful death.

The elderly man tries to speak again. Another thirsty, a woman with scraggly dark hair and patches of scalp torn out, also turns to look at me, followed by others. Only those who appear less decayed seem capable of forming words, their lips moving silently. I find myself leaning forward, as if straining to hear them.

I want to step back, to break away from their gazes, but I'm captivated, much like the night Donovan first held me with his mind. My body is transfixed, but my mind remains alert.

"No ..." a whisper echoes in my head.

"What the heck are they doing?" Tasha's voice startles me as she joins me, her gaze focused downward. She seems to have shaken off her earlier daze. The darkness acts like a curtain, highlighting the scene below. If it weren't for the thirsty gazing upward, I might have noticed Tasha's transformation from vulnerable to seemingly unafraid. But I don't question it, nor does it matter at this moment.

"I don't know," I reply, my voice barely a whisper. The young Asian man has detached himself from the group and is moving with a purposeful stride. Unlike the typical, erratic shuffle of the thirsty, his steps are steady, almost reminiscent of his human life. He reaches a wall and, after a moment's contemplation, begins to climb it with an eerie, spider-like agility.

"Oh, God."

In a panic, I jump back, pulling Tasha with me and slamming the balcony door shut. My breaths come in rapid bursts, my heart racing, eyes wide with fear.

I feel her shake off my hold. "Get off me," she snaps, pushing my hand away.

But my focus isn't on her. It's glued to the locked balcony doors and the ominous silhouette now on the other side. The shadow moves with an unnatural swiftness, a grace that should have vanished with death. Then, dropping from the railing, it lands on the balcony before rising to its full height.

"Run," I scream, terror lacing my voice. Whirling around, I dart towards the door, my hand gripping the handle, yanking at it desperately.

But Seth has locked us in.

CHAPTER
TEN

Trapt, with nowhere to run, the thirsty at our door is relentless and unyielding. It hasn't figured out how to open the door yet, but it's only a matter of time. My heart races, breaths coming in frantic gasps, each pulse a relentless drumbeat as the door rattles with increasing urgency. Panic claws at the edges of my mind, the world seeming to constrict around us.

Tasha stands beside me, her earlier contempt now overshadowed by the suffocating fear that grips us both. "What do we do?" she whispers, her voice thick with desperation.

"I don't know," I admit, as the ominous figure beyond the glass moves. Seth's warnings about their lack of intelligence feel like a distant memory. This one is different; it's learning, adapting, inching closer to breaking into our sanctuary.

Desperation gnaws at my core as I search frantically for another way out. We're trapt, defenceless, and the creature's crude attempts to unlock the door become increasingly frenzied.

"No," I gasp as the lock gives in and the door starts to

open. A shiver of dread courses through me as the creature, born of starvation and decay, slithers into the room, its features twisted into a nightmarish snarl.

Its eyes meet mine, and I refuse to look away. The rules of survival dictate never to be the first to avert your gaze. That's what my father used to say in business too. Looking away shows cowardice.

My trembling hand fumbles around for a makeshift weapon, anything. The room is a chaotic battleground of broken chairs and splintered wood, remnants of Donovan's rampage. My fingers curl around a jagged piece of wood, and I pull it in front of me, using it as a shield.

I thrust it out. "Stay back," I warn, even though I know the words won't stop this thing. It moves unhurriedly, circling us with predatory deliberation, biding its time for the right moment to strike. Seth is wrong. Intelligence gleams in its eyes, a primitive understanding of its desire and the calculated means to get what it wants.

"Stay right there."

The thirsty twitches, flaring its nostrils as if it can smell my racing heart.

"Keep it there," Tasha says.

Out of the corner of my eye, I see her moving. "Tasha ..." But she's stepping away from me, taking small, cautious steps. It's going to attack her ...

But no, it makes no move towards her. Its dull eyes are locked on me, and I maintain my unwavering stare, silently pleading with it to stay put. I do not want to be the damsel in distress, but right then, I wish Seth and Killian would come back.

It makes guttural noises, hissing and growling, but its words are devoid of any meaning.

· · ·

A CRASH BELOW, followed by shouting, shatters our silent standoff. Seth, Killian, and Naneve must have arrived on the lower floor, inciting a vicious response from the thirsty. Their screeching and hissing reach a fever pitch.

The creature takes a step closer, lips curling back to expose its fangs. I grip my makeshift weapon tighter, bracing for a desperate defence.

Tasha, standing in front of the glass box, her face a mask of determination and fear, suddenly lunges at the creature with a wooden leg in hand, bringing it down onto its back. The creature hisses in response, its fury evident as it turns to confront her. She leaps back just in time to evade its clawed swipe. Seizing the opportunity, I strike its head with my stick. The blow is solid, but it only dazes the creature.

The door to the room bursts open. Tasha has opened it – she must have had the key all along. Our eyes meet briefly, but before I can react, she's gone, slipping out and closing the door behind her, leaving me alone with the thirsty .

As the creature lunges at me, I push a table toward it, sending it crashing backward. It's dazed, its brief moment of cognitive clarity dulled.

I scramble for the door, bursting into the corridor and jerking it closed behind me. Tasha is gone. The corridor is shrouded in darkness, with only the faint green glow of an exit sign for guidance.

The thirsty smashes against the door, trying to break through. As I reach the door leading to the stairs, it opens, and not just one, but three of them emerge, snarling and clawing. In panic, I run, desperately seeking an escape. I manage to open the door to another corridor, but a gnarled fist slams into my back, sending me sprawling. With a desperate swing of my weapon, I connect with the creature's head again, a wet crack sounding as blood splatters the wall. I scramble away and into a new room flooded with light.

Seth must have reached the office because the lights fully come on. It's not sunlight, but it still hurts their sensitive eyes. Yet, the woman accompanying them shields her eyes, a behaviour that shouldn't be possible.

They're thinking.

CHAPTER
ELEVEN

The room is suffused with the unmistakable reek of blood and death, the lingering scent heavy in the air. The constant hiss of the thirsty forms an unending roar that surrounds them.

Killian stands guard at the door, his chest heaving with each deep breath. The effort of keeping the creatures at bay is evident in his every movement. His clothes are marred with blood, his blade stained, and smears of gore are splashed across his face – a warrior who's been through war.

Naneve mirrors his appearance and posture. Her wide eyes are a testament to the horrors they've just faced. Her hair is stained with blood, and her weapon is splattered with the remnants of her own gruesome battles. Bits of flesh cling to them, tattered and torn.

Seth's clothes bear the marks of the fray too, with tears in his sleeves and the occasional claw mark on his skin where the odd thirsty caught him. As he presses the buttons, the machines spring to life with a series of clicks and hums.

Donovan.

Everything has been intentionally turned off, not just the main switch but the auxiliary controls as well, in a deliberate effort to ensure the thirsty and any other threats from outside can breach the sanctuary.

At least Donovan didn't destroy the panel – that's about all Seth can think. He had half-expected everything to be smashed to pieces, leaving them trapt. Of course, Seth never voiced that fear when he ordered the descent. All he could do was hope.

As the cannons outside fire their red mist, they hear the thirsty outside screeching. The sound is a piercing echo in Seth's brain, scraping along every crevice of his mind. But they'll back away soon. They'll chase the dead blood, sate their insatiable hunger, and then lay down and die, waiting for the sun to claim them in the morning.

The three of them listen for a while, letting the hum of the fading frenzy peter out.

Killian breaks the silence, his voice heavy with tension. "This will clear them out? They'll leave?"

Seth nods, a glimmer of determination in his eyes. "It'll draw them out. Anyone who drinks will die, and those who don't, we can finish off ourselves."

THE LIGHTS FLICKER ON, illuminating the room in a harsh, bright white light that reveals Seth's true condition. He can usually pass for human, masking the redness around his eyes, but now it's impossible to hide. His skin is unnaturally pale, and his eyes are a deep crimson, a stark reminder of his vampiric nature. The effort has taken a toll on him, his head swimming, as if he's on the verge of slipping away into unconsciousness.

"Sire ..." Killian's voice, laced with concern, breaks through as he steps closer to Seth, leaving Naneve to stand guard by the door.

"I am alright," Seth insists, bracing his hands on the table as the machinery of Skin Trade hums back to life, fulfilling their purpose – protecting those within its walls, creating a safe haven from the harshness of the world outside.

"You don't look alright," Killian counters, but Seth raises a hand to stop him.

"I need to get to the library. It's in the original foundations of this place," Seth says, his mind fixated on a specific book on its stand in the safe. He knows it's gone, taken by Donovan.

"What do you need from there?" Killian asks.

"Something that could mean life or death for us all," Seth replies absently, playing with the ring on his finger – a relic from centuries past, pulsing with a power that seems to have dimmed, not in light, but in feeling.

"I need both of you to go back to Payton and Tasha, check if they're okay. I will go to the library myself, and depending on what I find there, we'll decide our next steps."

Seth's mind is clear on the priority: to ensure Payton's safety above all else. Then, he'll focus on retrieving the book. Donovan can't use it without the ring, and certainly not without her.

"I can come with you, and Naneve can go back to the women," Killian suggests, eliciting a look of disgust from Naneve.

. . .

"Or you can go with them," Naneve interjects. "I am more than capable of assisting him."

Seth raises a hand again, the effort visibly taxing him, but it effectively silences any brewing power struggle. "There is no argument here. You both secure the women. I will follow." He moves towards the office door and releases the lock. The thirsty should be dead or dying by now. Even from inside the office, the silence is telling. When he opens the door, he isn't surprised to see most of the creatures outside, succumbing to the mist.

The few remaining thirsty are feasting on bodies already there. On a normal night, the guards would have shot each one of them for daring to come this close.

With a nod to Killian and Naneve, Seth prepares to leave, but then stops abruptly. A tingling sensation runs up his spine, causing the hairs on the back of his neck to stand on end. He tilts his head upwards, his gaze tracing the balconies and windows above.

"Killian ..." Seth's eyes darken to a deeper red.

Killian follows his master's line of sight and his eyes widen. "How the hell did they get up there?"

In response, Seth rips the remnants of his shirt, revealing a dark tattoo of black wings across his back. With a rising motion, they come to life, peeling out of his skin and stretching far and wide, sleek black feathers unfolding. "Meet me up there."

Killian races towards the stairs. Seth fans out his wings and pushes against the air to take flight, but nothing happens. Dread tightens in his chest as he watches the thirsty climbing the walls. Two of them dangle precariously from the edge, their grotesque limbs slowly pulling them up. He glimpses another slipping over the balcony, and a knot of fear forms in his stomach.

Payton.

Frustration and terror for Payton's safety consume him. He lets out a raspy call to his wings, willing them to work, but they refuse to obey. Breaking into a flat-out run, he heads to the wall, scrambling. Fatigue and pain are cloaked by the adrenaline coursing through his body.

SETH HAULS himself up the wall with a desperate urgency, his wings providing just enough lift to prevent a fall but not enough for full flight. He lunges from balcony to balcony until he reaches the one where Payton should be. Spotting a thirsty trying to climb over the railing, he grabs it and throws it back down. Another one is already there, which he dispatches in the same manner.

"Payton?" Seth shouts as he bursts through the door. The room, flooded with light, shows Layla still lifeless on her back, but neither Payton nor Tasha are there. One thirsty lies on the floor, its head split open. The door he had locked is now shattered. Panic surges through him, but deep down, he knows she can't be dead; he would feel it.

Racing out into the corridor, he finds it well-lit, with blood marks along the walls. "Payton," he calls, trying to mentally reach her, but his thoughts are muddled, his body uncoordinated.

"Seth ..." A voice, filled with panic and pain. He hones in on it, following the bloody handprints along the wall. He reaches another stairwell where more thirsty are ascending, their movements oddly controlled.

Seth leaps upward, relieved as his wings propel him powerfully through the floors. He finds Payton a couple of floors up, fending off the thirsty with a makeshift weapon.

They're not attacking her outright but stalking her,

watching, waiting for the right moment to strike. She's backing up the steps, one hand on the railing for support, narrowly avoiding a trip.

He flaps his wings, attempting to push through the thirsty, who surprisingly try to push him away rather than attack. They seem fixated on her. Seth backs away to gain momentum, then launches into a brief flight, landing on a railing close to Payton. A thirsty, its face rotten and hands mangled, strikes at him, hissing through broken teeth.

One of them manages to hit Seth squarely in the chest, sending him tumbling backward through the stairwell railings. He falls several floors before catching himself on a rail. The fall doesn't deter him but fuels his resolve. He must reach Payton, no matter what.

WITH SWIFT AGILITY, Seth pulls himself to his feet and scrambles up the stairs. He lunges at the thirsty that pushed him, his hands reaching for its head in a frenzy of determination. In a brutal move, he tears the head from its neck, ending its threat. Another thirsty swipes at him, intent on getting him out of the way.

Amidst his formidable power, Seth is haunted by a memory – a day long ago when he couldn't reach Payton in time, her cries and screams echoing in his head. The memory fuels a desperate panic in his chest; he can't let that happen again. He can't endure losing her twice. He was human and powerless then, but now, he is a force to be reckoned with.

Letting out a roar, Seth throws himself towards the thirsty nearest to Payton. He attacks with ferocity, using his teeth and strength, lifting them and tossing them down the stairs. But still, they come, their focus undeterred.

Seth's presence, rather than scaring them off, drives them into madness, making them more desperate for Payton. She screams, fighting to keep them at bay. The elevator doors ping open, and Killian and Eve burst out. Killian swings his blade at one of the creatures, but they seem to come from every direction. One lunges at Payton, knocking her back.

She scrambles on her hands, trying to create distance between her and the creature. It relentlessly crawls towards her, unfazed by her kicks and shoves. Seth battles through the swarm of hands pulling him away, trying to reach her, but they overpower him, trying to toss him down as he had done to so many of them.

The creature is over her, and she desperately pushes its head back, her hand under its chin, fighting with every ounce of her strength. The situation is dire, with Seth struggling to get to her side, and the thirsty unrelentingly advancing. The room is a chaotic battleground, each of them fighting for survival against the overwhelming odds.

Payton screams at the thirsty, the wooden leg falling from her grasp as she tries to fend off the creature. She slaps her hand against its chest, holding it at bay as it snaps and snarls, inches from her face. Then, there's a sudden blast of air and an electric sensation that makes every hair stand on end, followed by a pop that resonates inside their heads.

Seth flinches, automatically covering his ears.

In an instant, the thirsty no longer bears its grotesque appearance but transforms into a young girl with deep red hair and perfect green eyes. She collapses onto the stairs, a heavy exhale escaping her lips. A tear rolls down her cheek before she closes her eyes and takes a final breath.

This unexpected event gives the group a moment of reprieve. Many of the thirsty are already dead, cut down by Naneve and Killian's blades or torn apart by Seth, their bodies thrown down the stairs. The few that remain put their hands up and shield themselves as if warding off some unseen light. They scramble away, now fighting each other for the doors in their desperate escape.

Naneve stands close to Payton, her own blade in hand, her breathing laboured from the exertion. She voices the question that lingers on all of their lips: "What the hell did you do?"

CHAPTER

TWELVE

All eyes are fixed on me, their gazes locking onto mine with a judgement that feels like an accusation of the gravest sin imaginable. Naneve's words echo in my mind, a relentless taunt. *What have you done?*

What have I done? I'm left grappling for answers, feeling overwhelmed. It's reminiscent of the time with Nico, when that Nostro attacked us and we were cornered. I had glimpsed inside him, seen the twisted path that turned him into a monster – his father's betrayal, his lost lover, his death....

"I saw her," I say, the words tumbling out, barely coherent but undeniable. I did see her – her life, her essence.

I step back, distancing myself from the bodies of the thirsty they've killed, strewn around me. My eyes settle on the lifeless form of the woman before me, no longer the snarling creature that had lunged at me. She looks about my age, her attractiveness accentuated by the blonde hair framing her face.

"You saw her?" Naneve's voice loses its usual sharp edge. This isn't a moment for disdain but for urgent conversation. "Explain. What do you mean you saw her?"

Finding my voice, I start to unravel the vision that had enveloped me. "In my mind, when I touched her ..." I pause, frowning, my hand lifting to my face as if to focus on the image. "She was a nurse. Dressed in dark blue hospital attire, a tunic and pants, tight around the waist, ending just below her knees. She was walking through a car park to her car, checking her phone. A little boy appears on the screen, maybe four or five years old. His joy at seeing her is clear. 'When are you coming home, mummy?' he asks, and they share a moment of laughter. She heads to her car and realises her keys are missing from her pocket. Fumbling in her bag, she finds them, clicks, and the car's lights flash, signalling it's unlocked."

My voice carries the heavy weight of this haunting revelation and the dread of what's to come.

"She slides into her car, tossing her bag onto the seat beside her. After ending the call with her son, she leans her head back, closing her eyes for a moment of respite after an exhausting day. What she doesn't know is that he's been lurking in the shadows, waiting by her car. Before she has a chance to react, he emerges ..."

The muscles in my throat tighten, and I press a hand to my mouth, as if holding back the words can somehow alter the tragic end of her life. I fix my gaze on her lifeless form before me, struggling to reconcile the image in my head with the reality laid out before me. My eyes lift to meet Seth's intense scrutiny.

"He waited for her and then took her life," Seth states, his voice tinged with a mix of understanding and sorrow.

"Yes," I whisper, the word scraping like shards of glass through my throat. "He killed her, turned her into one of the thirsty, robbed her of her life, her family, her future." My voice wavers, and the sting of unshed tears threatens to spill over. I mourn for her, for the son who lost his mother, for a family left to grieve. I don't know how, but I feel their loss deep within me, an ache that resonates with every fibre of my being. "This is what the virus does, what vampirism does. It robs you of everything."

I force a breath through the tightness in my chest, trying to steady myself amidst the chaos.

"You see the moment they die?" Seth's question echoes in my ears. I frown at him, not out of confusion but from the effort of making sense of everything happening around us.

"I have only seen death twice—" I pause, meeting his eyes again. I want to tell him about seeing his life, about how different it is with him, but I hesitate.

Naneve interrupts, thankfully redirecting Seth's focus. "What is she?" She's addressing me, her tone tinged with both curiosity and suspicion. "Something's going on here, right? She sees their deaths, and the thirsty are drawn to her. We opened the door on the floor below, and not a single one paid us any mind. They looked at us, yes, but normally they would have charged. They would have been all teeth and claws, determined to get to us. Not one of them came for any of us. Not even you."

"Because you are not a threat," I say, my voice quiet but certain. Somehow, I know this to be true. My mind feels like it has opened, unlocked something I can't yet fathom.

Naneve's gaze intensifies, probing, as if trying to

uncover the truth beneath my words. She's attempting to understand me, but the reality is I don't even understand myself. Guilt wells up in my chest, and I feel the urge to apologise, though I'm not sure for what.

Killian, usually silent, cleans his blade and sits on a step, his watchful eyes on me. His presence feels protective and curious, causing me to shift my gaze away, uncomfortable under his scrutiny.

Sensing my discomfort, Killian stands. "What's next on the agenda, Sire? We need to leave this place." His words seem to relieve Seth too.

Seth holds my gaze for a moment longer, an intensity in his eyes that feels almost tangible. I can trace every line of his face, the stubble on his jaw. My throat tightens as I wait for his response, expecting him to probe further as Naneve did.

But then he breaks our gaze and stands. "The library. After that, there's nothing left in this place for us."

"But this is Skin Trade," Naneve says, a hint of sorrow in her voice.

"Bricks and mortar, a mere backdrop for my business dealings," Seth responds, his gaze sweeping the aftermath around us. I wonder if he's looking at the lifeless bodies or seeing beyond the walls. "We'll proceed to Shadow Holme and I'll contact Lucius. I trust he's taken all those not present here to safety."

CHAPTER
THIRTEEN

Perched on a grand chair in the centre of the room, Donovan exudes an air of regal authority. The chair, resembling a throne, is strategically placed to allow him a commanding view over those brought before him. The only missing symbol of his power is a crown, one that metaphorically adorns his brother's head.

As he stares out the window, rolling a silver coin deftly across his knuckles, his gaze is sharp and penetrating. If looks could travel distances, Seth would be dead – a mistake Donovan regrets not rectifying long ago.

He inhales deeply, his nostrils flaring slightly. Dwelling on past misjudgments serves no purpose now, after centuries of rivalry.

The door swings open, causing the vampire guard to step aside quickly. The guard catches the door with grace, bowing as Amelia saunters in, a blood-stained cloth pressed to her nose.

"Is that all you're going to do? Just sit there?" she challenges, stopping short of fully entering the room. The blinds are open, allowing sunlight to filter in, enough to make her hesitant to advance further.

When Donovan remains silent, Amelia raises an eyebrow, placing a hand on her hip. "Hello? Are you asleep?"

Slowly rotating the chair with his foot to face her, Donovan speaks, "Is the boy still alive?"

"Yes, he's still alive. Why else would I am bleeding like this?" she retorts, gesturing with the bloodied cloth. Donovan smirks, seemingly amused by her discomfort. "If you expect me to stay awake during daylight, I need something more substantial."

Vampires are bound by the ancient rule to sleep during the day. Seth, Donovan, and even Amelia are no exceptions. Ignoring this rule leads to bleeding from their noses, eyes, ears, and eventually, internal haemorrhaging. But Donovan has noticed a curious change since biting Payton – he doesn't bleed, nor does he feel the same pull of the dawn.

"Do you ever tire of complaining?" he asks dryly.

"I'm not complaining. I just need something else," Amelia insists.

"Did the boy give you anything?"

Though she is still made, her smile turns wicked, her eyes gleaming darkly. "No, but I believe he's close to confessing anything we want." She snorts. "He has no idea where your precious Payton is."

Donovan sighs, his disappointment evident. "That's a shame."

Amelia doesn't care. She runs a finger under her eye, revealing a streak of red. She extends her bloodied hand towards Donovan. "Look at this. You stand in the sunlight, unfazed, while I fall apart over this girl ..."

"We do this for all of us, even Marcus," Donovan says.

"Even Marcus?" Amelia scoffs. "Do you think he's suffering for you? No, he's comfortably asleep while I'm here with you, as requested."

"You'll get your reward," Donovan assures, stepping back towards the window. Sunlight streams in, bathing the table in a warm glow. He boldly places his hand in the sunlight, an act that should have seared his flesh but mysteriously doesn't.

Amelia stares at Donovan, her mouth hanging open in disbelief. The tantalising promise of a life in the sunlight, of reclaiming the experiences she lost in her human life, is the sole reason she aids him.

"Bring me Jonathan," Donovan commands, directing his order to the vampire guard by the door. This guard, a female vampire, appears to have been in her forties at the time of her turning. Her dark hair is laced with streaks of grey, and her face bears delicate lines, remnants of the ageing process she once underwent.

"Sire," the guard nods respectfully, casting a fleeting glance at Amelia before exiting.

"See," Donovan remarks, "She knows her place."

Amelia's lip curls in disdain. "If you think I'll ever bow to you like that, you're sorely mistaken. The only one bowing here will be you." With a defiant gesture, she steps forward, allowing the fabric of her dress to part along the split, revealing her long, bare leg. Her hand glides teasingly down her thigh.

Donovan turns away from her seductive display, uninterested.

"You used to be fun," Amelia taunts.

He nods, a hint of nostalgia in his voice. "I used to be many things."

Jonathan strides into the room, accompanied by the

vampire guard. He walks with his own volition, stopping before Donovan with a presence that radiates power and dignity. He stands as an equal to Donovan, a status Donovan himself had bestowed upon him.

Humans are so effortlessly manipulated.

"What is it that couldn't wait? I was in the middle of an important meeting," Jonathan inquires with a hint of irritation.

"Your lawmaking?" Donovan asks, a teasing smile playing on his lips.

"Some of it, yes." Jonathan's role is crucial — crafting laws for the humans. It's part of their alliance, vampires and humans together, striving for equality and ensuring atrocities like Alitora never arise again.

"I need a woman," Donovan states plainly, almost disinterested. .

Jonathan gestures towards the vampire guard by the door. "There's one right there."

"No, I need a human woman."

The look of confusion and realisation that crosses Jonathan's face nearly sends Donovan into laughter. He can only imagine what Jonathan thinks he needs a woman for. But in truth, Donovan doesn't yearn for such things. Amelia satisfies his needs when she's not acting entitled. And then there's Payton, the one who Donovan believes will fulfil every desire he harbours.

"Why do you need a woman? You said ..."

"It's not for me," Donovan says. "Amelia is on the brink of bleeding all over your exquisite furnishings. I'd prefer she didn't turn into a puddle of blood on your floor. She needs to feed."

"Feeding, but I—"

"You're blubbering," Donovan cuts in sharply. "Choose

someone whose absence won't cause too much trouble. We wouldn't want to disrupt those precious laws you're drafting."

Jonathan might have protested or said something more, but Amelia's piercing gaze silences him.

"I don't want a woman," Amelia says firmly.

"You get too distracted by any men," Donovan retorts. "You need to feed, so you'll accept whoever Jonathan provides. And if he fails to deliver, feel free to feed on him instead." His smile is predatory as he heads towards the door.

"And where are you going?" she asks.

"To consult an old friend. If Nico doesn't have the whereabouts of Payton, perhaps Crevan will."

CHAPTER
FOURTEEN

I have no idea what Shadow Holme is or who Lucius might be, but Naneve and Killian both nod in understanding as Seth moves with a sense of purpose. We've come away from the stairs, leaving the thirsty locked in the stairwell. There's no light that can touch them there; no windows in that space. Rot and decay will see the end of their bodies, but only the woman I touched has returned to what she was before. The others remain in their decaying states.

Maybe it's an illusion or some magic that binds them to their monstrous forms.

Seth's eyes are a deep red again, his wings retracted. His chest is marred with the blood of those he's killed. We follow him through the maze that is Skin Trade, moving in silence.

"What are we looking for?" I finally muster the courage to ask.

"A book," Seth replies, but he offers no further details.

I wonder what could be so special about a book, but

Killian and Naneve seem to know. They say nothing as we continue.

"Are you sure he has the book, Sire?" Killian asks.

"I am certain. You saw him at the Summers' residence. My brother is incapable of such feats. What he has become is not of this world, and there is only one source for that transformation," Seth responds with conviction.

"Then why are we checking?" Naneve questions.

"Because I need to be certain."

We descend the staircase, moving through the winding labyrinth of doors. The building is deep, built into and onto the cliffs—a baffling arrangement of doors, windows, and hallways, an underground cavern of mystery and intrigue.

Finally, we reach the bottom, and I dare not look back at the dizzying descent we've made. Every surface appears sculpted from the most delicate materials, each level leading to a corridor, the entire place eerily silent with locked doors. It feels like something out of a fantastical tale, filled with enchantment.

But the true marvel unveils itself when we reach a level dominated by grand metal gates. They stretch from floor to ceiling, adorned in shades of black and gold. The opulence is striking, and I feel the atmosphere tighten around us, as if all oxygen has been sucked out of the air. We stand, transfixed, gazing at the gates where Seth is looking. On the floor lies a lock, and it is broken.

CHAPTER
FIFTEEN

With a grunt, Killian leans into the heavy gate, pushing it open. The hinges creak with disuse. Stepping inside, he flips the light switch, and the room is bathed in a warm yellow glow. Despite the illumination, shadows cling to the corners of the vast space, as if they have gathered there for decades on end.

The shelves, built into the walls from floor to ceiling, are crammed with books in every conceivable colour, from vibrant hues to neutral shades and everything in between. Some spines are so old they're falling apart at the seams, their covers tattered and held together by mere tendrils of cloth.

I can't help but gasp in amazement. I feel like Belle in 'Beauty and the Beast', exploring the palace library. All those books, just waiting to be read. I yearn to sift through them all.

My awe is quickly shattered by the heartbreaking sight at the centre of the room – books strewn haphazardly across the floor, their pages torn out and shredded by claws.

"Quite the ... display," Killian comments grimly, stepping closer and nudging the books with his foot, causing their pages to flutter. "Did he have some kind of rage attack?"

Seth's expression remains inscrutable, but his eyes, intensifying in redness, betray the truth. "Jealousy is a dangerous emotion."

Without making any effort to pick up the scattered books, Seth strides forward, his scarlet gaze scanning the room. "Rowena," he calls out, his voice reverberating through the space, echoing off the walls and bouncing back from the lofty ceiling. I'm not sure who he's searching for, but the urgency in his voice intensifies as we move deeper into the library, navigating the labyrinthine shelves, an endless sea of words.

We round a corner, and I stifle a gasp, quickly covering my mouth as if to suppress the horror.

"Rowena—" Seth rushes toward the woman before us, his voice a mix of distress and shock.

"Oh, God," I whisper, feeling a surge of nausea in my throat. My stomach churns as I avert my gaze, but the horrifying image is already seared into my mind. She's seated in a chair, deep crimson rivers running down her chest, dripping onto a shattered teacup on the floor beside her. Her head is tilted at an unnatural angle, her throat gruesomely slashed. The tendons are so brutally severed it's as if she's nearly been decapitated.

Seth stands silently before her, staring down at her lifeless body. The only evidence of emotion is the hardening of his jaw, a subtle yet powerful display of his inner turmoil.

. . .

Killian's observation cuts through the tense atmosphere. "Donovan has gone mad."

Seth slowly shakes his head, a mixture of sorrow and resignation in his movement. "I wish that were the reason. At least then, we could find some rationale for his actions. But this is just my brother." He exhales deeply, his nostrils flaring as his gaze shifts from Rowena's body to the vault with its door slightly ajar.

Curiosity pulls me towards the vault, the destruction within evident. Objects and books lie scattered on the floor, and metal covers lining the walls, resembling safety deposit boxes, are dented and clawed through.

"It's gone," Naneve says, her voice tinged with realisation.

Seth's attention is drawn to a box lying on the polished floor. He approaches and crouches down. Another book, open and displayed, lies within it. One page bears a savage knife wound, as if someone had plunged the blade deep into it with force. Seth's reaction is subtle yet intense, his fists clenching.

My stomach churns, my breath catching. I recognise that book. I've seen it before, in a dream, a vision of Donovan and a woman they fought over—a life from centuries past. That was her book, and I am certain there is more to this tale than I know.

Seth rises, his head bowed, then furrows his brow, his gaze locking onto me. "Where is Tasha?" he suddenly asks, as if he's just realised her absence.

I freeze at his unexpected question. My throat tightens as I recall Tasha leaving me to the thirsty, possibly intending to let them kill me to save herself. Despite wanting to think the best of people, I know the painful truth. "She went to find you, to get help," I mutter, avoiding Seth's gaze.

The colour drains from Seth's face as he stares at me. His silence is unnerving, his gaze piercing as if reading my very thoughts. Hesitating, I brace myself for his reaction, but he simply nods solemnly. "We'll find her, get Layla, and leave this place."

Gathering my courage, I ask, "Aren't there others here?" In my mind, Seth, being a king, must have subjects, followers. His domain shouldn't be empty.

Seth's response leaves a heavy silence in its wake. "There is no one here now, save for the dead."

I find myself staring at him, thinking back to when I was first with him, when he took me from the auction. My mind drifts to the auctions, where we met Amelia. There was hostility, anger in her demeanour toward Seth, and he was dismissive of it. I wonder about the dynamics of their relationship, even though it's not my place to delve into such matters. Yet, I can't help but ponder.

"Lucius and Arabella will have taken everyone to safety," Killian explains, as if I should know who they are.

"Lucius and Arabella?" The names are unfamiliar to me, but then, why would they be? I'm just a former slave, and this world is far beyond what I knew.

"They are ..." Killian pauses, glancing at Seth for permission. When Seth doesn't object, he continues. "Arabella is Seth's firstborn, and Lucius is her protector, a wolf, not a vampire."

"They will have taken everyone to safety when my brother attacked," Seth adds. "The dead here are mostly patrons of Skin Trade, unfortunate souls caught here on the night Donovan threw you from the balcony."

"They fled?" I blurt out, my tone unintentionally accusatory. I'm ready to fall to my knees, asking for forgiveness.

Seth answers without taking offence. "None of them would be a match for my brother if he decided to harm them, especially not if he has the book."

"They have been slaughtered," Killian interjects somberly.

"My blood flows through their veins, and my blood is of his blood. That alone affords him some semblance of control over them. And that is my mistake," Seth admits with a heavy heart. "One I hope they have not paid for with their lives."

CHAPTER
SIXTEEN

The climb back up the steps is arduous, each step steeped in silence and sorrow. It reminds me of the times I was taken out of the basement in Craven's place, the dread and fear thick in the air, feelings that tended to fade as we became accustomed to the routine.

Seth, Killian, and Naneve keep their thoughts to themselves, shrouded in their own contemplations. Their silence is a stark contrast to the usual dynamics of our group.

The protective formation around me is unmistakable, even though Seth never explicitly requested their protection. It's a tacit acknowledgment of the danger that still lurks around us.

Eventually, we emerge onto the main floor, a scene of carnage that, despite having witnessed it before, still takes my breath away. The overwhelming loss of life leaves an ache in my chest. This place, once alive with music and crowds, is now a tomb to countless lives wasted in a war whose purpose seems increasingly unclear. What are we fighting for? Each other? The world itself? I wonder if anyone truly knows.

In the elevator, the sight of a half-eaten body on the floor, a victim of the thirsty, is a gruesome reminder of the night's horrors. We enter the room where Layla lies behind the glass, still in whatever state Seth has put her in.

"Tasha isn't here," Naneve notes, looking around the room. We thought she might return here after failing to find Seth, but she's nowhere to be seen. I never believed she would be, but I hadn't voiced my doubts.

"Find her," Seth instructs Killian and Naneve. His gaze lingers on me as he continues, "Assure her she is not in any trouble."

I stop breathing. Any doubt I had about him not knowing I lied, evaporates But, strangely, I don't want Tasha to suffer. Despite her leaving me, I hold no anger towards her.

Killian and Naneve leave to find Tasha, and Seth's attention returns to Layla. "Is she asleep?" I ask, though 'sleep' seems an inadequate term.

"She is in her death-sleep," Seth replies, working the control panel to unlock the door. We both wait, and I can't help but wonder what would happen if Layla suddenly sprang up, attacking as she had tried before. But she remains still.

I stay on the other side of the glass, moving closer to observe Seth and Layla. He tenderly brushes her hair away from her face and whispers something in her ear. The way he looks at her, with a paternal affection, makes me wonder about the others he's turned, like Arabella. Did they choose this life, or were they forced into it?

Knowing the woman on the stairs hadn't gone willingly to her fate weighs heavily on my mind. The complexities of

Seth's world, its rules and customs, are still a puzzle to me. When I think of Seth, it's almost easy to forget his status among them – a king. But what does that truly mean?

Seth's gaze locks onto mine, and I feel the electricity between us. His power envelops me, dark yet gentle, drawing me in despite my urge to step back. The realisation that only the strongest vampire could be king sends a shiver through me as I ponder the true extent of Seth's power.

"How will we take her with us?" I ask, referring to Layla. His stare unnerves me, but I'm also acutely aware of his nature.

"She will come with me in my car. Killian will take you on his bike, and Naneve will take Tasha," he replies softly. "If she wakes while we travel, I want her to be with me so she doesn't cause you any harm." He steps out of the glass box but leaves it open. "We must move swiftly, for the night won't last forever, and I don't want to be on the road when the sun rises."

"If we move in the dark, won't the thirsty come after us? More precisely, me?" The thought of them descending on us fills me with dread, and I doubt our ability to fend them off outside.

Seth steps closer, and I flinch, but he gently lifts my chin with his finger. His eyes are now a deep blue, infinitely deep. "You're scared again," he observes softly.

I try to deny it, but my words falter with him so close. "Not afraid of them."

He holds my gaze a moment longer before stepping back, allowing me to breathe again. "We'll stay on the road through the city. That will keep us safe from them. Once we reach the border, there won't be so many of them. They just want something to eat. They won't go out of their way to get that."

"My heart is beating faster now," I whisper weakly.

Seth seems to notice my discomfort. "Nothing to hunt," he reassures me.

Suddenly, the door opens, and Naneve enters with Tasha, gripping the other woman's arm tightly. Killian follows, his face expressionless.

Tasha's eyes dart between me and Seth, likely wondering if I revealed what she did. Part of me wants her to feel the fear I felt when she left me, but another part feels pity.

Seth steps closer to Tasha, his height towering over her. She swallows hard, her breathing hitching. "It was foolish of you to think you could find help by seeking me out," he says sternly.

Tasha stammers, searching for an explanation. "There were too many of them ... I'm sorry, I—"

"You certainly will be," Seth responds softly, his tone not reflecting the harshness of his words.

Turning to Killian, Seth outlines the plan. "We must leave now if we are to make it to my home before sunrise." He describes who is going with whom and other details that I don't fully grasp, but they do, and that's all that matters.

As I watch them, they look every bit the fighters they are, prepared for whatever lies ahead in the night.

CHAPTER
SEVENTEEN

Seth carefully carries Layla to his car, placing her in the back seat with a gentleness that contrasts his formidable appearance. As I approach to help, he gently pushes me back "It is better you maintain distance."

Despite my desire to help, part of me yearns to touch her, to ensure she's okay. Layla was kind and gentle to me, sacrificing herself to protect me from Donovan. I feel a sense of duty to return that kindness, yet I'm powerless to do so. I do as he says, and keep back.

Naneve and Killian, with Tasha in tow, have gone to retrieve their bikes, leaving me at the entrance of Skin Trade's car park. The car park is quieter than usual, a silent testament to the lives lost here tonight. I can't help but notice a few cars parked, likely belonging to patrons who will never return.

I can see the doors on the main part of the foyer. A few people stop by a look inside, some dressed in gowns and suits, others in very little. The world carries on as if nothing has happened—vampires and humans living together, slave and master—and for some reason that shocks me. I remember feeling the same when my mother died. It seems odd to me that everyone would just carry on as normal skin. Skin Trade is closed, in darkness. Everyone inside it, dead or running for their lives, yet the world moves on.

It feels like a dream.

Lost in thought, I think about Seth and Donovan, their complex relationship, and then my mind shifts to my father and the unresolved issues there. My head feels cluttered with questions and uncertainties.

"What are you thinking?" Seth's quiet voice startles me from my reverie.

Hesitantly, I answer, "I was thinking about Nico." My voice lacks conviction, betraying a shadow of fear. "Do you think your brother will kill him?"

Seth's response is sombre. "I would like to tell you for certain he is safe, but Donovan is capable of anything." His words send a chill down my spine.

The sound of motorcycle engines breaks the tension. The distinct rumble of the bikes signals Naneve and Killian's return, and the street instinctively clears a path for them. Their presence, once harsh and barbaric to me, now seems a necessary part of this new world I'm learning to navigate. Seth has opened my eyes to realities I never understood, and while it's still alien to me, I'm gradually piecing it together.

It's Killian's voice that cuts through my thoughts. "I managed to get Des on the radio. The place has been secured, and they're waiting for your orders. It should hold for now, but she wants to move them, especially the women with children."

Des is Dessie. A woman I met at the Death Bringers

compound. She was the one who gave me the clothes I now wear. *Look after these,* she'd told me.

I think I owe her an apology.

Seth nods in response, his gaze firm and focused. "I'll provide them with instructions tomorrow. Tonight, we rest."

CHAPTER
EIGHTEEN

As darkness descends, the city awakens to its nocturnal pulse. Vampires emerge, mingling with those who adore them and those who yearn to be like them.

Donovan strides through the throng, an air of disdain surrounding him. To him, humans are like vermin — the longer he lives, the more this sentiment festers. They seem to destroy and corrupt everything they touch. Despite his own destructive past as a human, for which he harbours regret, he believes he has evolved since his transformation.

The streets buzz with human activity, mostly gravitating towards the various clubs and establishments. Donovan observes the hypocrisy: humans who once scorched the skies to oppress vampires, who unleashed afflictions like HIV and Alitora, now freely mingle in these dens, offering their blood as if in a twisted celebration.

But their actions are not without self-interest. They desire, they beg, confirming Donovan's belief that they need to be controlled. Left unchecked, he fears they will lead the world to ruin, ensuring no one, vampire or human, survives.

Donovan strides through it all with an air of disdain that's palpable even amidst the chaos. He's tall, dark-haired, and exquisitely handsome; his eyes a fierce red that seems to burn holes in those who dare to look at him for too long. But it doesn't stop them.

His tailored suit fits him like a glove, accentuating every muscle and curve of his body. He oozes power and control as he weaves through the crowd, his movements graceful yet purposeful - he knows where he's going and doesn't have time for frivolity. Everywhere he goes, women smile at him, their cleavage provocatively displayed, their movements flirtatiously calculated. Each one seems eager to capture his attention.

The vampire elite mix and mingle with the pulsating crowd, their regal presence commanding the attention of all those around them. Glimmering jewels and luxurious fabrics adorn their immortal bodies, reflecting the intoxicating lights of the city. They feed off the energy that surrounds them, a feast for their senses as much as blood is to their sustenance.

Donovan continues through this dazzling spectacle, resolute and unimpressed. Maybe another night he'd have paid one or two some attention, taken what they offer to him, but tonight he has other ideas, a different person he needs to see.

Crevan.

Crevan is exactly where Donovan expects to find him — at his bar, Nocturne. It's his usual haunt.

Unlike the others who queue patiently, Donovan doesn't pause at the entrance. The vampires staffing the bar recognise his stature immediately. They open the doors upon his approach, their actions verging on a bow, acknowledging his presence with a silent respect.

Donovan straightens his shoulders and adjusts the cuffs of his jacket, ensuring his appearance is impeccable. He moves with purpose, well aware of his destination. The table in the back corner, always surrounded by a select crowd, is his target.

Pushing his way through the burgeoning crowd, Donovan ignores the distractions around him. The dancers on stage, the explicit displays of flesh and desire – while it's all available and has often been his for the taking, tonight he remains focused. His gaze is fixed on the table where Crevan holds court.

Crevan, draped in brocaded silk and fine velvet, lounges like a king among his courtiers. His ebony hair cascades down his back in thick, lustrous waves—an intriguing contrast against his pale skin that glows with an internal luminescence exclusive to their kind.

He's pathetic. A shambles to their kind.

The sight of Crevan laughing with the women around him sets Donovan's blood aflame—an irony not lost on him

As he approaches the table, the air thickens. A hush falls over the previously raucous crowd as all eyes follow his progress across the room. The music dwindles to a faint background noise as everyone awaits the imminent confrontation.

Crevan looks up from his wine glass and meets Donovan's gaze with a cryptic smile playing upon his lips. He extends one arm out in invitation while signalling for another round of drinks with the other. Despite his ostensible hospitality, it's clear to Donovan that this isn't a gesture of goodwill—more like merry jest before the storm.

"Can I offer you something to drink?" Crevan asks, his

eyes glancing not towards the bar but at the assortment of humans nearby. Some willing to offer their services, and the odd one who isn't.

Donovan doesn't spare them a glance. "You were supposed to keep her with you," he states, cutting straight to the point. "She was meant to stay here until I decided otherwise."

Crevan, a high-ranking vampire in his own right, wields significant power and commands respect. Yet, in the presence of Donovan, his authority is diminished. He maintains a composed facade, careful not to show fear before the surrounding humans and vampires, but he's also wise enough not to overstep his bounds with Donovan. "Perhaps we should discuss this in my office," he suggests, making a move to leave.

Donovan shakes his head firmly. "I'm not here for a conversation. I want to know why you defied my orders. Why was she put up for auction, and how did my brother end up with her?"

"H-he offered to pay," Crevan stammers, a hint of hesitation in his voice.

"Pay?" Donovan echoes, the single word slithering from his lips like a viper poised to strike. His eyes, iridescent against the low light of the room, fixate on Crevan. The crowd draws back. "And was it your right to sell her?" Donovan hisses. Crevan's eyes widen slightly at this blunt confrontation but he quickly recovers, hiding his surprise beneath a mask of deceitful calm.

"I didn't have a choice," Crevan protests weakly, avoiding Donovan's gaze by refilling his wine glass once again. Both vampires know that he's skirting around the truth. "He threatened—"

"He threatened you?" Donovan interrupts sharply, "Or did he simply offer more?"

"Such matters are better spoken about in private."

"No. I strongly disagree. You thought you could betray me? You believed I would simply accept everything as fine?" Donovan's voice cuts through the room, filling it with a palpable, oppressive silence. The tension thickens, almost tangible.

Crevan swallows audibly, his fingers tightening around the glass in his hand until the stem cracks, breaking into two pieces. "Donovan," he starts, his voice wavering, a feeble attempt to regain some control. But his efforts crumble under Donovan's relentless, piercing glare.

But before Crevan can further plead his case, Donovan reaches into his jacket, swiftly drawing a small, unique weapon. It resembles a hybrid of a crossbow and a pistol, with a ball of light at its centre. A collective gasp echoes through the room, followed by a whimper at the sight of this weapon – a daylight gun, its bullet not just deadly, but horrifically so, carrying the essence of the sun's rays.

Without a second thought, Donovan aims and pulls the trigger. The bullet tears through the air with an ear-splitting crack, blazing a scorching path across the table, and striking Crevan squarely in the chest.

Crevan's face contorts in unimaginable agony, but Donovan is beyond empathy. Crevan had one task – to keep her away from Seth, and he failed. The encapsulated rays of daylight burst forth from within Crevan. Even he can't suppress his cry of pain as it echoes through the room. The crowd backs away, huddled together, watching the horrific scene unfold but offering no assistance.

Crevan's body convulses on the floor, the powerful figure now writhing in excruciating agony. Smoke rises from his skin as the lethal daylight effect takes hold, his dark hair fanning out as he claws desperately at his chest. It's a macabre dance under the dim lights, culminating in a final, silent thud as Crevan's struggle ends.

His lifeless body lies on the scarlet carpet, a gruesome halo of blood pooling around him. The crowd recoils in horror at the sight.

Amidst the chaos, Donovan stands unflinchingly, his face emotionless, cold, and distant. He gazes down at Crevan's lifeless form, an air of finality surrounding him. His icy eyes betray nothing but the deadly determination that manifested tonight.

"Let this serve as a lesson," Donovan announces, his voice resonating through the stunned silence. "This is the fate of those who dare cross me."

CHAPTER
NINETEEN

We zip through the streets, the city's illumination casting an eerie glow that seems to keep the thirsty at bay. Despite the darkness, the artificial daylight creates an odd semblance of safety, a stark contrast to the lurking shadows where the thirsty hide, their hunger an almost tangible force.

I find myself drawing closer to Killian, gripping his waist tightly and pressing my face against his back. The sight of the thirsty, so visible yet untouchable, haunts me. My mind races back to the nurse and her last night, leading me to ponder the fates of others like her. Once ordinary people with lives and families, they now exist as mere shadows, consumed not just by vampirism but by something far darker, a pervading sense of despair in this transformed world.

The transformation of the world is so striking. Since my last venture into it, the change is so drastic it feels almost unrecognisable. Alone, I would be utterly lost in this new, divided landscape. Many blame the virus for this division, but in truth, it's the people—humans, vampires, and others

—who have fractured it, letting it spiral into chaos and ruin.

I can't help but wonder about the future of this place. What will it look like in another decade? Will it still exist, or will it have succumbed completely to the darkness that seems to be encroaching ever closer?

The streets are bustling with activity – people, cars, bikes, even limousines. Seth navigates through the traffic with a sense of command, a clear sign of his authority in this world, and Killian follows suit with equal confidence. Tasha and Naneve trail behind us. A glance back at them sends a shiver down my spine, their stares piercing through the night, so I quickly refocus on the unsettling scenery around us.

The night unfolds like a dystopian tapestry, a world where the lines between human and supernatural blur into a harrowing new reality. And in this world, I find myself clinging to the one stable element I have – the presence of Seth and his protectors – as we cut through the night, heading towards an uncertain future.

As we journey across the border, the city's radiant lights gradually fade, giving way to the enveloping darkness. Shadows along the roadside shift eerily, reminiscent of liquid darkness. Despite the presence of more day light, casting their protective glow to repel the thirsty, the surroundings feel markedly different. Roads, like the one we ride, form a network connecting vampire cities and towns, an interconnected web linking places like Skin Trade to the rest of this transformed world.

This landscape is a far cry from my childhood memories. Buildings that once stood proud are now derelict, their skeletal frames jutting against the skyline, leaving rubble where thriving communities once were. I can't help but ponder the existence of others like Killian and Naneve, the Death Bringers, in other hiding places like the Hollows. Jackie, the leader of the Hollows, who was willing to kill me, I question our understanding of this world. Were we wrong in our assumptions?

As we continue, the landscape morphs again, sparking my curiosity. I sit straighter on the bike, holding tightly, eager to see more of this world. Despite being warned against it, I've always harboured a curiosity about the world beyond my confinement. The mantra of "stop hoping, stop thinking" never quelled my desire to see beyond the life of a bonded slave.

Ahead on the road, three figures catch my eye. I hesitate to call them people, knowing they are no longer human, but anything less feels like an injustice to their former lives. It's important to remember who they were before becoming these creatures. Their existence now seems so unfair; if it were me in their place, I'd yearn for someone to end my suffering.

One of them steps boldly onto the road, directly in the path of Seth's car. The headlights cast an eerie glow, making its eyes shine like beacons in the darkness. Startled by the light, it quickly retreats, but not before lashing out at us, hissing its displeasure.

Killian, alert and ready, swiftly reaches for the blade holstered at his hip. With practised ease, he unsheathes it, positioning himself for a swift and effective strike as we approach the creatures. They move towards us, arms outstretched, their gait accompanied by an unsettling sound that blends a ghastly inhale with a scream. The noise pierces my ears, making me wanting to cover them.

As we ride past, Killian swings his sword, decapitating two of the creatures in one fluid motion. Blood spurts in a grotesque fountain from one, collapsing to the ground, while the other stands momentarily headless. Naneve, following closely behind us, ensures the third creature meets a similar fate, her actions causing it to collide with the second, both crashing to the ground in a heap.

For as long as I can, I keep my eyes fixed on the fallen creatures until darkness swallows them, and they fade from view, becoming part of the night once more.

We ride onward, the sky gradually lightening with the soft hues that herald the approach of dawn. The air is crisp and cool against my skin, and I tuck my fingers into Killian's coat for warmth, the chill causing my knuckles to tingle. Killian's back serves as my only shield against the cold wind that strikes my face.

Seth occasionally glances in his rearview mirror. Sometimes our eyes meet, and in those moments, it feels as if he's peering deep into my soul, as if nothing else in the world exists but him and me. It's a feeling that's both chilling and exhilarating, igniting a warmth in my heart—a heart I thought had long since ceased to feel.

Hope used to be a part of my life when I was younger. Hope for me. Hope for my father to find me, hope to escape, hope for the world to change and hope for something to get better.

Now, as we ride through this altered world, I find myself clinging to that same hope, albeit different. It's a hope not just for survival, but for something more, something beyond the confines of the life I've known.

The night when Craven sold me at the auctions, despite its horrors, was perhaps the best night. I could have never imagined a world like this, even though our journey has been fraught with fights and battles. But there's something about the way Seth looks at me, something I can't quite put into words or perhaps even comprehend. It's like he can touch me even when we're several feet apart. It's akin to the part of me that senses the thirsty all around us—this part feels his presence, too. But he carries a deep sadness beneath his darkness, a sorrow hidden beneath the cocky and controlling exterior that he presents to the world.

We've veered off the main road onto a series of other roads. I'm disoriented, my head spinning, and I'm exhausted. I can't even recall the last time I slept. My eyes sting with weariness, my back throbs and my hands ache from gripping onto Killian.

Seth's previous observation about this area proves accurate. We come across very few of the thirsty here, the landscape offering no refuge or sustenance for them. The few buildings we pass are nothing but dilapidated ruins. I find myself wondering about the humans who might be hiding within these structures, much like Jackie and the Hollows, desperately trying to avoid both the thirsty and the vampires. The sense of desolation is thick, reminiscent of a post-war city where everything is shattered, and everyone has vanished.

After encountering the initial three, we only meet about half a dozen more thirsty. They are mere stragglers, aimlessly wandering along the roadside, forlornly searching for their next meal. But we are not their prey. Killian and Naneve efficiently end their miserable existence, swiftly and without hesitation. Their actions, though harsh, seem almost merciful in this desolate world where the line between predator and prey is so thinly drawn.

As we continue our journey, the stark reality of this new world becomes ever more apparent. It's a world where survival is a daily struggle, not just for humans but for all creatures caught in this changed landscape. The emptiness and ruin around us serve as a constant reminder of the fragility of life and the relentless march of time that spares no one in its wake.

As we move into the dense woods, darkness envelops us. Seth somehow maintains his speed, navigating through the thick trees with a confidence that suggests he's travelled this path countless times. Clinging tightly to Killian, my heart races with anticipation, half-expecting a sudden collision with a tree or an unexpected tumble over a hidden branch. Their skillful manoeuvring through the forest is nothing short of remarkable.

My heart leaps as we come upon a massive grey wall, partially hidden behind the trees and hedges. The bare trees, devoid of foliage, resemble skeletal silhouettes with bony fingers stretching over the brick, adding an eerie touch to the landscape.

Seth eventually brings the car to a halt in front of a large gate, and Killian, Naneve, Tasha, and I stop behind him. When the gate opens and we drive through, and it feels as though we're entering a different world. The driveway winds gracefully, meandering through meticulously maintained lawns, walls adorned with vibrant flowers, and purposefully placed trees. It's a stark contrast to the desolation we've left behind, reminiscent of the grand estates from my childhood.

The path seems endless, and for a moment, I doubt there's anything at the end. But then, a large, beautiful house comes into view, standing majestically amidst its splendid grounds. As Killian pulls to a stop behind Seth's car, I take in the building's grey brickwork and dark wood-framed windows, lights glowing warmly in various rooms. It seems to promise a bustling interior, perhaps full of staff.

Removing my helmet, I shiver as the cold air envelops

me, but my attention is captivated by the grand structure before us. The mansion's door swings open, and a man, appearing to be around sixty, steps out. His human appearance surprises me. He descends the steps, bowing gracefully to Seth as he steps out of the car.

As the man addresses Seth, I'm struck by the tone of respect in his voice, a stark contrast to the command and authority often associated with Seth's interactions. "Seth," he says, acknowledging our presence, "I see you've brought guests."

Seth responds with urgency, "Yes, and one of them is injured. Theo, can you prepare the cold room? We need to get her inside before the sun comes up." His concern is evident, a different side of him that I haven't seen often.

Theo's eyes briefly scan the car where Layla lies before nodding in understanding. He turns to us, his bright blue eyes flicking over to me. I feel an odd sensation under his gaze – not fear or judgement, but something else, an inexplicable familiarity. His attention returns to Seth. "Elena has a pot of stew on the stove. I assume your guests are hungry?"

Seth, looking down at his shirt with a frown, seems out of place in his dishevelled state, contrasting sharply with his usual pristine appearance. "Hungry and tired. Have you heard from Lucius?"

"I have, Sir. He informed me of the situation. We've been expecting your visit."

As I dismount from the bike and hand the helmet back to Killian, a tightness grips my throat. Panic sets in as I feel an invisible constriction around my neck. My hands rise instinctively to scratch at my skin, gasping for air.

My vision blurs with panic, and I stumble backward, crashing into Naneve. I struggle for breath, my lungs and throat burning as though constricted. The world spins, and my heart races, pounding a frantic rhythm in my chest.

"Payton—" Seth is suddenly before me, grasping my arms, his presence both grounding and overwhelming. My vision blurs, and I'm torn between wanting to push him away and needing his support. I drop to my knees, burying my face in my hands, desperately trying to draw in air. It feels as if I'm drowning, my lungs starved of oxygen.

For a fleeting moment, my mind escapes the present, whisking me away to a different place, a different time, as if I'm trapt in a memory or a vision, disorienting yet vividly real.

Confronted with the image of Donovan, my mind reels in terror. His face looms before me, grinning menacingly, the shape of his jaw so similar to Seth's but more severe, his eyes piercing.

"Where are you?" he taunts, his words seeming to float on his breath, chilling me to the core.

"No ... I can't ..." I whisper, panic-stricken.

"Payton." I hear my name called from a distance, but it's as if I'm trapt, unable to reach out to the voice.

In desperation, I curl into a ball, pressing my hands against my head, trying to push Donovan's image away. I shake my head, and gradually, his image fades, releasing me from its grip.

"You can't hide like this," the fading image of Donovan taunts.

My eyes snap open, and I'm back in the gardens, gasping for air. Seth is on the ground beside me, concern etched on his face, while Killian and Naneve stand nearby. A woman, presumably Elena, is in front of us.

Coughing and wheezing, my body desperately sucks in

air, my throat burning painfully. I'm disoriented and weak, my entire body trembling from the ordeal.

"What did you see?" Seth's voice cuts through the haze, not asking what happened, but focusing on what I experienced.

I stare at him, my throat dry and voice hoarse. "Donovan," I manage to croak out.

Seth's jaw works tightly, a sign of his own inner turmoil. He nods slowly, then turns his gaze to the woman, Elena.

"He knows," Elena states, her voice carrying a weight of certainty.

Seth nods in agreement. "And he has her book."

CHAPTER
TWENTY

Confusion swirls within me as I feel their eyes on me, intense and searching. "What's going on?" I demand, more forcefully than I ever would have dared with Crevan. Is it stupidity or a newfound comfort? I've spoken my mind to Seth on many occasions and have yet to face any retribution. I don't stop, either. "What is happening to me? With this?"

"We should get inside," Seth says, casting a glance towards the ever-lightening sky. The sun is rising, heralding a new day.

And I feel it too - an inexplicable sense of change, a shift in the very air around me. It's as if the dawn is not just bringing light to the world, but also to the murky uncertainties clouding my mind. There's a part of me that yearns for answers, for clarity amid this chaos that my life has become. As Seth turns his back on me and walks towards the car, I feel something deep within me crack, like a fissure opening in the core of my being.

"Why won't you tell me? What's with all the secrecy?

You all have these secrets," I call out, my voice a mix of frustration and desperation.

The others remain silent, observing the unfolding scene. Killian looks at Seth, his expression one of a child awaiting a response from an authority figure.

Seth peers over his shoulder at me. "You're not ready," he states bluntly. Then, dismissing me, he nods to the man he called Theo. "Carry her inside. She shouldn't wake, not with the sun rising. Put her in the cold room, have a bag of blood beside her, then lock the door. Make sure it is secured."

"Sire," Theo bows, his one word signifying acquiescence to Seth's orders, and he sets about his task diligently.

Seth walks to the other side of the car, retrieving items he gathered from Skin Trade before we left.

I step away from them, feeling a surge of independence. Seth gave me my freedom; he said so himself. When I tested it, he never chased me. That's what's on my mind now as I watch them, my questions unanswered, my voice unheard.

With Crevan, I learnt to suppress everything, to not let emotions swamp me. Even when I felt them brewing inside, I learnt control. Now, watching these people moving about, knowing things I don't, hiding things from me, it's almost too much to bear.

Killian seems to sense what's on my mind, and my need to just walk away, even if only for a little while. Maybe to go somewhere I can think, somewhere away from all the chaos to unpack all the facts. He angles his head towards me, lowering the bag he's holding. "Payton..."

I shake my head, feeling my resolve slowly waning. "I'm sorry." In that moment, the need to escape, to find a space where I can breathe and think clearly, becomes overwhelming. I don't know where I'm going, but the urge to distance myself from the unanswered questions, the secrets, and the overwhelming sense of being controlled is all-consuming. I take a step back, turning as I do, and before I fully comprehend my own actions, I run.

Driven by a flurry of emotions, I find myself running not away from the property, but deeper into its vast land. Even amidst my emotionally charged escape, a part of me knows better than to venture beyond its boundaries. So, I aim for the trees, veering off the path, just getting away from them.

It's a turmoil inside – hurt feelings, things I have no right to feel, or so I tell myself. It's about Seth. I can't quite unravel the connection between us, but it's there, palpable and frustrating. He and I are on opposite ends of this world; he wields all the control, and I have none. Yet, there's this inexplicable pull in my chest, almost like a betrayal, that he won't speak.

As I dash through the underbrush, I can hear them behind me. Killian's cautious call, "Sire," echoes faintly. But he isn't coming after me.

Seth calls my name, and I shake my head, refusing to stop. Then his voice again, firm and commanding. "Get the others inside." Yet, he doesn't chase me, either. He just calls out from the edge of the woods.

I'm not sure where I'm going. The adrenaline courses through my veins, propelling me forward. My legs can't move fast enough, my arms pump to drive me onwards, but it feels like it's not enough.

In this frantic escape, it's not just the physical distance I'm trying to put between Seth and myself. It's the emotional distance, a desperate attempt to gain some semblance of control over the overwhelming feelings that are threatening to consume me. The confusion, the frustration, the unspoken bond – it's all too much, too fast.

The forest around me blurs as I push through, branches snapping underfoot, leaves rustling in my wake. My heart pounds in my chest, echoing the tumultuous rush of my thoughts. With each stride, I'm not just fleeing from Seth and the others; I'm running towards a clarity I desperately seek, away from the shadows of the unknown that loom over me.

Eventually, my pace slows as my legs begin to protest, my arms ache, and my chest heaves for air. I come to a gradual stop, bending over with my hands on my thighs, allowing myself to inhale deeply, trying to steady the ragged breaths that fight to escape.

Exhausted, I drop to my knees, leaning forward to rest my face in my hands. I'm not crying or sobbing; I'm simply existing in the moment, allowing myself to just be.

Sitting there, with the cool earth beneath me and the canopy of trees above, I feel a small measure of peace. It's a respite from the chaos, a momentary escape from the complexities that have entangled my life.

I close my eyes, taking in the sounds and smells of the forest. It's a stark contrast to the world I've been thrust into. Here, there are no secrets, no veiled truths, or unspoken bonds – just the simplicity of nature, indifferent and beautiful in its indifference.

In my disoriented state, I find myself in what seems at first like a clearing, where the foliage has been cut back. As I get to my feet, pushing up off the soft earth, I take a closer look at my surroundings. For a moment, my troubles are forgotten, replaced by a curious urge to explore this unexpected find. I step forward, my eyes scanning the area. It slowly dawns on me – this isn't just a garden. It's a graveyard.

There are headstones, five of them, all lined up in a

somewhat haphazard manner. My pulse steadies as I take in the sight. The headstones are old, crumbling away in places, weathered by time. Most of the inscriptions have been eroded, their stories lost to the ages. But one catches my eye, standing out from the rest. It's been cared for, the letters perhaps recently re-carved into its stone surface.

"Katherine," it reads.

I whisper the name aloud, "Katherine ..."

The name hangs in the air, a silent echo in the stillness of the graveyard.

I sense Seth's presence before I see him; his aura is unmistakable – warm yet commanding. "She was your wife?" I venture, lifting my eyes to meet his.

He stands near a large tree, an unexpected casualness to his posture, hands in his pockets. "No, I never had the chance to marry her," he answers, and his voice carries a weight of sadness that resonates with me. "You're running away again?"

Taking a deep breath, I feel a sense of calm seeping in, easing the urge that drove my flight. "I don't know," I admit, aware of the tension in my body as he steps closer. A part of me braces for a reprimand.

"I know you're looking for explanations. It seems like we're keeping secrets from you.

"Because you are," I say instinctively, not holding back. "It feels a lot like…" I pause, trying to hold back my words, but they spill out regardless. "Ever since you bought me, it's been nothing but secrets and conflicts. It's been about people wanting something from me or deceiving me. Your brother, Killian, Naneve. It's …" My voice falters unintentionally. "Everyone seems to want something from me or dislikes me, and I don't understand any of it. When I ask, no one gives me straight answers."

"We will," he assures me.

"No, you won't. I don't understand what's happening. I see these visions, hear voices, and it feels like you all know, but back at the house ... What was that just now? What happened back there? You all know something, and no one tells me anything. I'm expected to just... just..." Words fail me, unable to fully express the turmoil inside. "

He steps closer, and I notice his glance shifting between me and the headstone. "It's complicated."

"You say that, but maybe I'll understand," I counter, holding his gaze. Our eyes lock, and in that moment, a silent communication passes between us. It's a mix of his hesitance and my insistence, an unspoken acknowledgment of the complex world I've been drawn into and my growing need for truth.

His top lip twitches slightly, revealing the edge of his fangs, a reminder of the supernatural world he belongs to. "What you just felt is magic," Seth reveals, his voice carrying a note of earnestness. "A kind of magic my brother doesn't know how to wield properly."

"Magic?" The word feels strange, almost surreal, on my tongue.

He nods in confirmation. "Like I said, it's complicated. There's much for you to learn, but it has to be in your own way and on your own time."

"But I will learn it," I say, a determination settling within me.

"Yes."

"The magic, it's connected to the book he stole?" I ask, trying to piece together the fragments of this intricate puzzle.

"Yes."

I look at him, feeling the weight of his gaze as I process

this new revelation. Finally, I ask, "What is the book your brother took?"

He nods, the seriousness in his expression deepening. "A grimoire."

"A grimoire? What's that?

"A witch's sacred book. A book of magic and life passed down witch to witch."

I frown, puzzled by the situation. "But you're not a witch."

"No, I am not," Seth confirms.

"Then why do you have this grimoire, and why does your brother want it?" My curiosity grows, along with a hint of frustration at the complexity of it all.

He pauses, as if carefully considering his response. Then he exhales slowly. "It was given to me a long time ago, when I was first turned and filled with a desire for vengeance." This revelation about Seth's past, his transformation against his will ... Was he like the woman? Like the man?

"By a witch?" I ask, trying to piece together this intricate puzzle.

"Yes," he replies.

"But why? If it's sacred, why would she entrust it to you?"

"Because I needed it," he says, his voice laced with a hint of mystery.

"That sounds like more riddles," I say, my tone reflecting my growing impatience for clarity.

Seth looks at me, a solemn expression on his face. "It was given to me to care for, so when the rightful owner came into my path, I could hand it over," Seth explains. "My brother has taken it because the magic contained within it is immensely powerful. In our hands, it's potent, but in the hands of its true owner, that magic surpasses anything we've known in this world. My brother desires it to ascend to power, to control our kind."

I stare at Seth, trying to process the enormity of what he's revealing. "That's how you became king? Because of that book?"

"The magic within it granted me abilities I never sought," he admits, a hint of reluctance in his voice. "I fear it's the same magic that has empowered my brother in the ways we've witnessed." Seth glances upwards towards the trees, where the sky is visibly brightening, the hues shifting with the dawn. "Come back to the house with me. Rest. The sun is rising."

Seth extends his hand towards me, palm up, a gesture that seems to bridge the gap between us. In this moment, he isn't just the centuries-old existence vampire, but rather a man, someone with depth and an untold history. For reasons that escape me, I find myself drawn to him, sensing a connection that goes beyond the surface.

I glance to Katherine's grave before taking his hand. It is her eyes I keep looking through and I don't know why.

CHAPTER
TWENTY-ONE

We hurry our pace through the trees, heading towards the house. Seth moves with hard, purposeful steps, casting wary glances at the slivers of sunlight piercing through the gaps in the tree canopy, where leaves fail to completely shield us.

"I thought you could walk in the sun," I say, trying to keep up with his brisk pace.

He nods, his voice strained. "The sun is too hot."

His height and long strides give him an advantage, and I struggle to match his speed. As we move, I see his face. "Seth, you're bleeding." Blood oozes from his nose and ears, adding urgency to my steps as I try to catch up with him.

He seems to falter, staggering slightly as if overcome by sudden weakness. He steadies himself against the trunk of a tree, not stopping but visibly struggling to maintain his balance.

Panic sets in. We have to get to the house – and fast. The sun, which seemed so benign to me, is a lethal threat to him. I don't understand the change, but there is no time to ask.

"Oh, god," I mutter under my breath, fear and concern for Seth propelling me forward. The urgency to reach the safety of the house becomes paramount. I push myself to move faster, ready to offer whatever support I can to help him make it back before the sun's rays inflict more harm. "Lean on me," I urge, sliding up beside him and extending my arm to bear his weight.

Seth, stubborn and independent, shakes his head and pushes off from the tree, attempting to make it on his own. But his strength falters; he drops to one knee and then the other, his hands clutching at the grass. Blood now drips from the corners of his eyes.

"Seth …" My voice is a mix of plea and worry.

In a spur of the moment decision, I take off the thick jacket Killian gave me before I got on the bike. It's not mine, too big for me, but it had offered protection. Now, it's Seth who needs protection. I drape the jacket over his back, creating a barrier between him and the harmful rays of the sun.

"Lean on me," I say again, more firmly.

This time, Seth accepts my help, taking shelter under the cover of the jacket as we emerge from the trees into the garden area. "Help," I shout, my voice reaching its peak, a desperate scream for assistance. "Someone help me."

The others, having followed Seth's earlier orders, have already gone into the house with Tasha. I'm alone out here with Seth, trying to get him to safety.

My heart pounds in my chest as I half-carry, half-drag Seth towards the house, his weight leaning heavily on me. Every step feels urgent, a race against time and the sun's merciless rays.

The front door of the house seems miles away, but I press on, my shouts for help echoing unanswered.

"Anyone." My voice is a mix of panic and desperation as we approach the house.

Suddenly, the door bursts open. Killian, with Naneve close behind, races down the steps towards us. "What the hell happened?" Killian demands, his voice laced with urgency.

"Is he hurt?" Naneve demands.

Their faces register fear and shock as they reach us. Killian quickly takes Seth's other side, aiding me in supporting him. But as we move, the unforgiving sunlight catches Seth, and I watch in horror as blisters erupt rapidly on the exposed side of his face. His pain is palpable, and it tears at me.

Chaos surrounds us, a frantic scramble to get inside. Killian and Naneve help hustle Seth—and by extension, me—into the house, away from the deadly rays of the sun.

"What was he thinking?" Naneve chastises as we cross the threshold into the safety of the house.

"I'm sorry," I whisper, guilt weighing heavily on me. This is my fault. If I hadn't run away …

But there's no time to dwell on what ifs.

As we cross the threshold, Seth's condition worsens. He is unsteady, teetering on the brink of collapse. Killian, acting quickly, gently but firmly removes me from Seth's side. Seth sinks to his knees, and I stand beside him, filled with terror. "Seth—"

The door slams shut behind us as someone closes it, and Naneve rushes to close the window shutters, casting the room into darkness. The tense atmosphere inside starkly contrasts with the brightening day outside.

Seth's hands clasp onto the floor, and his entire body seems to quiver with pain. "Sire," Killian crouches before

Seth, his voice laced with concern. He rests a comforting hand on Seth's shoulder.

Seth keeps his head lowered, his dark hair burned away in patches, leaving raw, peeling skin exposed. "Sir," Elena, the woman I met briefly outside, approaches with a trembling voice. "Seth ..."

With Killian's assistance, Seth rises, revealing the extent of the damage to his face. An involuntary gasp escapes me as our eyes meet. Pain emanates from his eyes, and his face bears the cruel scars of the sun's embrace. Blisters mar one side of his face, his lips are swollen, cracked, and blood trickles from his nose and the corners of his eyes. Agony etches his features.

Something inside me stirs, a deep urge to go to him, to hold him. In this moment, I see two worlds intertwined – the present, harsh and painful, and the echoes of a life that isn't mine, a past that seems to connect me to Seth in ways I can't fully understand yet.

"Bene sum, mea cara," he says.

My reply comes automatically, and I don't know where from. "Semper bene me habeo cum tecum sum."

CHAPTER
TWENTY-TWO

We're in a spacious kitchen just off the main hall through which we entered. I sit in a chair in this room, a perfect blend of old world charm and modern elegance. It's as if Seth has merged different eras into one space. The walls are lined with rich, dark wooden panelling, giving the room a cosy atmosphere. Thick, heavy velvet curtains hide large arched windows, allowing only the dim light from wrought iron chandeliers, suspended from the high ceiling, to illuminate the space.

The centre of the room is dominated by an old-world, warm wooden table, evidently having witnessed countless gatherings over the years, adding character to the space. Surrounding the table is a mix of chairs – some intricately carved in an old-fashioned style, while others boast sleek, modern designs.

All eyes are fixed on Seth, mine included. The room is silent, charged with tension, until Elena finally breaks the silence. She moves to face Seth, her concern evident. "What on earth were you thinking?" she chides gently, cradling his face as if he were a child. She tilts his head to inspect the injuries. I wince at the sight of his blistered, raw wounds – injuries he sustained helping me, chasing after me. My fault.

"It doesn't matter," Seth says, trying to dismiss the concern.

"Like hell it doesn't matter," Elena scolds, shaking her head. Seth starts to rise, but Elena firmly pushes him back into his seat. "Stay there. You should be resting. You're no use to us in this condition. Without you, we have nothing."

Seth shakes his head. "You know what needs to be done."

"Aye, I do. And that's to mend the mess you've made of yourself," Elena asserts, taking charge. She attends to him with the care of a mother, her actions speaking louder than words. Her nurturing presence in the room brings a sense of order to the chaos, a reminder that even in this world of supernatural beings, human care and concern remain a powerful force.

My head still spins and I can't shake the memory of what just transpired I uttered, words that flowed effortlessly from my lips, though their meaning eludes me. I know them, though. I whisper them to myself once more, "Semper bene me habeo cum tecum sum." It's as if I can almost grasp the memories, but they remain just beyond my reach.

No one pays me any attention, except for Seth. His eyes lock onto mine with piercing intensity, and I see weariness and a hint of exhaustion he tries to mask. Then, shifting his focus back to Elena, he asks, "Have you spoken to Lucius?"

"I did. Donovan …" Elena replies, her voice steady. She's at the stove now, her movements both deliberate and focused. She stirs a large pot, simmering with a concoction so aromatic it fills the room. Then, she turns to a smaller pot, adding various herbs and mysterious ingredients. Each addition seems purposeful, and the air around her thrums with energy, an unspoken power emanating from her very being.

The scents mingle in the air, both comforting and exotic, creating a sense of anticipation. I'm struck by a realisation: Elena isn't human, at least not in the way Theo, Tasha, or I am. There's something different about her, but she isn't a vampire either. My thoughts drift to the grimoire Seth mentioned, the book passed down to witches. Could Elena be a witch?

Elena murmurs something under her breath in a language unfamiliar to me. The air in the kitchen shifts, becoming warmer, almost electric. The small pot bubbles, and she observes its contents carefully, her eyes reflecting the flickering stove light. "Theo, get something for them to eat while I tend to Seth," she instructs.

Seth closes his eyes, leaning his head back as if familiar with Elena's methods.

"What's your plan?" she asks him.

"To rest first. Everyone is exhausted," he responds, a hint of weariness in his voice.

"Including you?"

A wry smile crosses his lips. "Aye, including me." He opens his eyes as Elena gently applies a piece of cloth to his face, covering the areas where his hair is missing. He flinches slightly at the touch, indicating pain, but remains silent. She continues to apply the soothing cloth to his skin, stopping only when he speaks again. "My brother has the book."

Elena's gaze remains fixed on Seth, her unusual eyes searching his face.

Seth shakes his head, dispelling some unspoken thought. "Not the ring," he clarifies.

"So, he can't read it?"

"Not yet, but as you saw, he has managed to open its pages."

Elena's gaze shifts to me, and I can't help but be drawn to her eyes – not any ordinary colour, but a rich shade of purple. A cold sensation washes over me, as if the power in the room is reaching out, seeking me.

I pull my gaze away, feeling like I'm on the edge of a deep, dark pit, about to fall in.

Theo places a steaming bowl on the table in front of me, accompanied by a spoon and a hunk of bread. "Eat," he instructs gently and I am glad of the break. "It'll do you good."

Around the room, the others are already eating. Naneve leans against the kitchen sink, her bowl in one hand as she shovels soup into her mouth. Tasha sits at the table, gracefully spooning mouthfuls of soup.

Killian is beside her, dunking his bread into the soup with an urgency, as if afraid the food might be snatched away.

The soup is hot, the bread warm. I hesitantly pull off a small piece of bread and dunk it in, my actions unnoticed by the others.

This feels like a calm before the storm.

CHAPTER
TWENTY-THREE

By the time Donovan returns to the Summers' residence, his temper has escalated to perilous heights. But there is nothing at hand to vent his fury on, nothing to soothe his raging storm.

He storms through the house, his movements forceful and uncontrolled, slamming doors with such intensity that they rebound off the walls. Any sensible resident in the house will wisely stay out of his path.

He strides purposefully to the room housing the grimoire, the book that might hold the answers he seeks. Stopping just short of hurling the ancient book across the room, he flips it open, his movements rough and impatient. "Give me your answers," he demands, slamming his fist down onto the book in frustration, as though the force of his blow could compel the grimoire to relinquish its secrets.

Clutching the sides of the lectern, he bows his head, his fangs emerging in a physical manifestation of his inner turmoil. He lets out a primal scream, allowing the sound to rip from the depths of his being, echoing his inner chaos and desperation.

"Seth ..." His brother's name escapes Donovan in a guttural growl, laced with bitterness. Seth, who always takes, who always claims everything Donovan believes should rightfully be his.

Taking a deep breath, Donovan closes his eyes, attempting to quell the storm of fury within him. Yet, paradoxically, he feeds the anger, conjuring memories from a distant past when they were both human, when she belonged to him. These recollections, tinged with nostalgia and pain, only serve to fuel the fire of his resentment.

Donovan's jaw clenches tightly, a muscle twitching in his jaw as he observes the scene below. Katherine's laughter, light and joyous, is carried up to his window by a gust of wind, taunting him. He sees in Seth's eyes a passion he recognises all too well—the same fervour that once ignited within him at the sight of her.

The pain envelops his heart as he watches the scene unfold, feeling like a nightmare. Katherine's golden hair cascades down her back, bouncing with each giggle that slips past her parted lips. Her ivory dress contrasts starkly against the monochrome green of the garden, making her an unmissable presence.

In his hand, he holds the blade Katherine gifted him, a symbol of their promise when they had agreed to unite. A political alliance, yet they vowed she would be his in all ways. Now, he grips the blade tightly, allowing its edge to press into his palm, the sharpness biting into his skin. Blood begins to seep down, a stark reminder of the pain he feels inside.

Donovan's gaze, once tender and soft when directed at her, now hardens. A veil of brooding anger descends over his striking blue eyes, and he inhales sharply, his heartbeat thundering in his ears, echoing the torment consuming him. The anger spreads through him like wildfire, obliterating his rationality and magnifying his sense of betrayal.

Is there anything his brother won't take from him? Seth had already claimed their father's love, undeserved though it was, and now her ...

Donovan's vision blurs at the edges as he sees Seth's hand lingering on Katherine's waist, and he grits his teeth in suppressed fury.

She returns to her room later, clutching a book he had given her.

Donovan, sitting unseen on the stairs between their rooms, watches her intently. Her smile, the one she wears unknowingly, tells him all he needs to know about who occupies her thoughts. Her every move and laugh betrays her feelings.

Beside Donovan lies a small, folded blue gown, tied neatly with a ribbon. He glares at it, as though it's the source of his frustration.

His father's gathering later ... If not for that, he might have given the gown to someone else. Perhaps he would choose a different companion. Perhaps later, when everyone is distracted, he might slip away to find a common woman who would see only him, not Seth.

Grinding his teeth in irritation, he grabs the gown and descends the steps. He pauses momentarily outside her door before knocking.

"Come in," her soft voice invites.

Upon entering, he is met with her smile, a facade of innocence and surprise in his eyes as she peeks at him through the mirror of her vanity table. "I thought you were in town with your father," she remarks, pulling a brush through her hair.

"I was, but we returned earlier than expected," Donovan replies, his voice measured.

. . .

Katherine turns to face him, her hair cascading gracefully as she sets the brush aside, her smile still warm. "Did you manage to take care of all your business?"

He nods, his response nonverbal, his thoughts elsewhere.

"Is something wrong?" she asks, sensing the tension in his demeanour.

A twitch of his lip betrays his inner turmoil. Clutching the gown in his hand, he struggles to maintain composure, his breathing slightly laboured. He keeps his emotions in check, aware that any outburst would jeopardise his father's plans. This alliance, this obligation, is the sole reason he restrains himself, the only thing preventing him from dismissing her outright.

His father's needs come first. This union must proceed flawlessly, as Katherine's betrothal to the family's illegitimate son would be unthinkable. At least in this, Donovan finds a cold comfort.

"I've brought you a gown for this evening. My mother assures me it's quite fashionable," he says, his tone devoid of warmth. Instead of presenting it to her, he places it at the end of her bed, his gaze lingering on the fabric. A part of him yearns to retract the gesture, to take back the gift and deny her this small kindness.

She approaches him as she always does when he presents her with gifts, but this time, Donovan feels an urge to recoil, to create a distance between them. Despite this, he remains rigid. "Thank you," she says softly.

His jaw clenches; Donovan meets her gaze directly. "You smell like him," he blurts out harshly.

Katherine frowns, and she instinctively starts to retreat, but Donovan grabs her wrist, his grip painfully tight. Leaning in closer, his vision tinged with red at the proximity, his anger surges. "You dare to make a mockery of me and my family, after all we've done to keep you away from the bathhouses."

Katherine gasps. "You're hurting me."
He jerks her close. "Get used to it."

CHAPTER
TWENTY-FOUR

Despite my exhaustion, sleep eludes me. My head throbs with an intensity that feels like it might burst, and the weariness I feel offers no comfort. My eyes sting from a lack of rest, burning as if they're on fire. I've lost track of time since I last slept – has it been one day or two?

The last time I truly rested was on the hard floor of the Hollow's basement. Even then, it wasn't proper sleep. Nico had roused me from that uneasy slumber, helping me to escape before the others woke up. Just thinking about Nico hurts. It twists my stomach into knots, souring something inside me at the thought of what might be happening to him, what has already happened. I close my eyes, imagining him there, almost as if I can reach out and see him.

The mere prospect of Nico being hurt, or worse, torments me. The images haunt me. In my mind, I place him in a place like where his mother had kept me – dark, damp, the smell of urine in a bucket. I taste blood on my lips and feel aches in my body. I'm so tired …

I sigh heavily and roll onto my side, selfishly yearning for sleep to whisk me away from my own torturous thoughts and the anguish they bring.

If only this were all just a dream, a mere illusion I could wake from. But that would also mean leaving Seth behind. Where would I even wake up? Back at Crevan's place, still his plaything, or in a room in Seth's sanctuary, treated like a pampered little princess?

Lying here, the coolness of the cotton sheets beneath me offers a small comfort. Regret gnaws at me – I should've demanded Seth rescue Nico too, not just me. Nico, just a boy, had shown courage in helping me, defying his own mother. And what had I done in return? In my escape, I had left him behind, alone and vulnerable. This realisation, the acknowledgment of my failure to save him, is a bitter pill to swallow.

I abandoned him.

"I'm sorry," I whisper into the dark room, filled with regret. The light flickers around me, emanating from the fireplace Theo lit. Mesmerised, I watch the flames dance and listen to the wood crackle, the only sounds breaking the silence.

Theo had noticed my shivering when he led me to my room. "I'll light a fire for you," he'd offered. "These large rooms can get quite chilly with little activity." I initially declined, insisting I didn't need it, but Theo persisted, and I eventually stopped objecting. Maybe I am the spoilt princess Naneve accuses me of being. She never mentions it when Seth is around, but her cautious glances and contemptuous eyes don't escape me.

Naneve is out on patrol, defying orders to rest and sleep. She's adamant about ensuring safety, refusing to relax her guard. "What use is the king's guard if she sleeps and allows him to be slaughtered?" she had declared. And in her unwavering determination, there was simply no room for argument.

Killian had told her she could take the first watch, then he would take the next and she was to sleep then. "What good is a king's guard if she's too exhausted to guard him and he ends up slaughtered anyway?"

Tasha is down the hall and Naneve nearby.

Although I crave solitude, the silence feels strange, almost too isolating. My mind buzzes with thoughts, a tangled mess I struggle to unravel. And then there's Elena – I sense something different about her. She's unlike the thirsty, yet there's a similarity I can't quite define.

Lying in bed, I wrap the blanket around my waist and draw my knees to my chest. The room's darkness contrasts with the chaos outside. I feel as if I'm enveloped in night, despite knowing the truth lies beyond the walls and windows.

Compelled to see the outside world, I swing my legs out of bed. My bare feet touch the cold, hard floor, and I tiptoe to the window, where heavy black and red drapes shield the vast pane.

Peeking through them, the sun's brilliance strikes me forcefully. Its intense light blinds, showing no mercy to those beneath its scorching rays. The sky, an endless canvas of azure blue, radiates sheer brightness. The sun, a radiant sphere of light, dominates the sky with a merciless glare, threatening to incinerate anything daring to face it.

As I squint through the window, the sun's harsh rays force my eyes to water and cause a throbbing headache. I can't help but marvel at how the trees and flowers in this place have managed to thrive. Most vegetation withers under direct sunlight, turning into nothing more than skeletal remains.

The only time I had ever seen flowers thriving was in Craven's greenhouse, an artificial sanctuary where vampires and humans could mimic basking in natural daylight. Maybe Seth had implemented something similar at Skin Trade, a clever illusion designed to protect the flora from the sun's lethal touch while keeping us sheltered. It strikes me that vampires might maintain gardens not for the love of nature, but to ensure their food source – humans – remains comfortable and content.

Outside the grey walls, the sun's brilliance washes over the landscape, rendering it surreal and otherworldly. The fiery tendrils of the sun's corona create an ethereal halo, intensifying the aura with palpable energy. The sky shimmers with overwhelming heat, distorting the distant scenery into wavering mirages.

The thought of stepping out into the searing sunlight reminds me of the pain Seth endured when the sun caught him. My heart aches with guilt for having run out, compelling him to chase after me, leading to his burns. It's a constant reminder that my actions, despite being unintentional, often cause pain to others—a burden of guilt I carry with me.

I let the curtain fall back into place, sealing the room in darkness once again, leaving only the comforting glow of the fire as my companion. I turn away from the window, intending to return to bed and surrender to sleep. Perhaps exhaustion will overtake me, offering a respite from these heavy thoughts.

However, instead of heading back to my bed, I find myself drawn to the double doors. Opening one panel, faint light spills into the room from beyond, illuminating a bed and the figure lying upon it.

With a quiver of uncertainty in my gut, I tread through the dark room, guided by the dim light of the fire glow. The cold floor that once chilled my feet now offers relief as I step onto a soft, lavish rug.

Before me lies Seth, grounded in slumber. His eyes are closed, head tilted back, and his dark hair still glistens from Elena's treatment. The burns that had earlier marred his face are gradually healing, becoming less menacing. They even seem to accentuate his already handsome features, giving him a more chiselled look.

I can't help but wonder if Seth dreams during these moments of rest. Does sleep for a vampire resemble an abyss devoid of visions? Perhaps they drift into a state where time and consciousness hold no sway, a realm of nothingness with no awareness of their surroundings or actions. As I approach, he appears almost human, vulnerable, and a stark contrast to the commanding figure I usually see him as.

Seth's lips part slightly, revealing the tips of his elongated fangs—a subtle reminder of his vampire nature beneath the facade of humanity. He breathes in a slow, rhythmic pattern, imitating human respiration, though vampires don't typically require breath. His chest rises and falls gently, existing in a delicate balance between the human and vampire worlds.

I stand beside him, close enough to touch, yet I hesitate to disturb his rest. A logical part of me suggests returning to my own bed, but something holds me back.

As I begin to turn away, he stirs and reaches out, capturing my hand with his long, slender fingers, sending my pulse racing.

"I'm sorry," I stammer, my voice barely above a whisper. "I didn't mean to wake you." My voice trails off as our eyes meet. His intense gaze, a piercing window to his soul, speaks volumes more than words ever could. It delves into the depths of my being, igniting an undeniable sensation within me.

For a moment, we communicate in silence, our eyes locked. His grip is gentle yet firm, and I find myself unable to pull away from his touch. Instead, I stay, lost in the intensity of his gaze.

Finally, he speaks, his voice low and filled with a gravitas that sends shivers down my spine. "You need not apologise. I welcome your company."

A multitude of thoughts, questions, and emotions whirl within me, creating a turbulent storm. Despite this, I'm rendered mute under his penetrating stare.

Lowering my head, I pull back slightly from the intensity of our connection. He allows the distance but not enough to break our bond.

"You are overthinking again," he says. But now, the fear and uncertainty that once clouded my feelings around him have faded, replaced by an enigmatic allure.

"I have so many questions," I murmur softly. "But it's not my place."

His sigh could have been a reprimand, but it isn't. Still, I flinch, bracing for the worst. "When will you understand? I have granted you freedom. It is yours to keep."

Our gazes meet, and my heart races. "If you can give freedom, then you can take it away."

He rises to a sitting position, turning so his legs dangle from the bed's edge.

I try to withdraw my hand, but he holds it firmly. His

grip is unyielding, and his positioning leaves me standing between his knees. "Yes, I can," he admits.

Those words send a tremor through my heart. "You can make me do anything you want," I state, more a realisation than a question.

"What if I demanded you in my bed tonight?"

CHAPTER
TWENTY-FIVE

My heart pounds in my chest, and despite my best efforts, my mouth goes dry, rendering me speechless. The heat radiates from my cheeks, and in frustration, I bite my lip.

He laughs softly at my shocked expression, causing colour to flood my cheeks even more. Struggling for words, I'm lost in a whirl of emotions. He takes a deep breath and releases it slowly. "I would not make such a request of you," he says gently but firmly. "Your freedom is yours to keep. I gifted it to you."

My eyes widen as his words sink in. He smiles and brushes his knuckles against my cheek, sending warm tingles down my spine.

Sensing my hesitation, his gaze softens and becomes inviting. Gently, he tilts my chin up to meet his eyes. "You are safe with me," he whispers, so low only I can hear.

My heart flutters at his words.

"Why are you awake?" he asks. "If Elena were to find us, she wouldn't hesitate to punish us both."

I blurt out before I can stop myself, "You let her

command you." It's a test of the boundaries of the freedom he's given me. "She's neither a vampire nor your superior."

His laugh this time is devoid of mockery. "You tell her that." He pauses, his expression turning serious. "I owe her my life, and with that comes trust and respect."

I can't help but marvel at him.

"Speak your thoughts," he encourages.

"You are unlike any vampire I've ever known," I confess. "You possess immense power, yet you wield it with an uncommon kindness."

"Just because one has power doesn't mean they need to be cruel. I could choose that path, but what would it achieve?" he muses.

"The power lies in the choice?"

"Exactly. Life is about choices. If there's anything I've learnt in my long life, it's that. You chose not to answer my question about why you're awake."

"I couldn't sleep," I admit.

"Still turning everything over in your mind?"

I bite my lip again and meet Seth's gaze. I'm teetering on the edge of revealing everything, wishing I could understand even a fraction of it all. I'm about to mention Nico, my fear of him palpable, but something else slips out instead. "My father," I say.

I pause, but the silence doesn't swallow my words. I even put my hand to my mouth, as if to hold them back. Nico isn't the only thing on my mind; he's the distraction I use to suppress other thoughts. "My father was supposed to protect me, to rescue me. I believed he would. It was all I ever dreamt of."

I don't realise I'm crying until Seth gently wipes away a tear with his thumb. "I'm sorry," I whisper again, for what feels like the hundredth time.

"Don't ever be sorry for your tears," he says softly.

I hear the naivety in my own words. "I was a fool."

"To think your father would come for you?"

"Yes. I—"

"All fathers should step up and do what's right," Seth says. "Some do it out of obligation, while others are too swayed by their own wants and needs.

"I thought maybe he was dead. That's why he never came for me." I can see Seth understands the need for that hope in my words, and he nods.

"That might have been easier. You'll probably learn a lot about your father that you wish you hadn't. And about the world, too. I'm only sorry I can't protect you from it all."

I narrow my eyes at him. "I don't understand you."

He smiles. "You don't need to." Moving back onto the bed. I can see it's a struggle for him; he's tired, and the rising sun challenges any vampire. I wonder how he's still awake, how the day hasn't yet forced him into slumber. He pulls back the covers. "Lie with me. Maybe then you can sleep."

Before I accept his invitation, I frown at him, tilting my head. "Why aren't you asleep?"

"That is a question you're not ready to have the answer to," he replies. "Now come, lie with me. Sleep may be a small battle, but it's one we must face."

CHAPTER

TWENTY-SIX

I settle into bed beside Seth, resting my head on the pillow. As I close my eyes, trying to calm my racing thoughts, I find comfort in Seth's presence. The silence in the room envelopes me, and my eyelids grow heavy.

But I resist the urge to sleep. The thought of facing my dreams alone, without Seth, is overwhelming. The feelings of betrayal threaten to drown me, and I struggle to push them away.

Seth gently brushes the hair from my face, whispering, "It's OK to be angry, to feel what you feel, but don't let it consume you. You've been through so much. Don't let this be the thing that breaks you."

It's as if he's reading my thoughts, my emotions.

His hand finds mine, his touch becoming an anchor amidst the storm of emotions. I've felt this way many times before, but never with someone like him. It's always been with other slaves, victims of their kind. It feels like a betrayal, yet with him, it's different, always different.

His fingers lightly trace a path along my knuckles, and I

allow my eyes to close. Sleep washes over me, and I surrender to it, drifting away into the darkness of my dreams.

My dreams mirror reality's darkness.

I cautiously lift my skirt to walk, moving quietly. I need to leave the room and descend the stairs. Using a candle is out of the question, as someone might see me. I know Donovan and his father are away for the night, but I can't afford to be careless. There are enough eyes to watch and report on my every move.

The baroness is in her room, thankfully overlooking the fields and the forest instead of this part of their land. I slip through the kitchen and make my way down through the vegetable patches where potatoes and carrots grow. The season is changing, and soon everything will need to be harvested.

I don't require light to navigate this path; I've done it countless times before, almost by muscle memory. I'm heading to the small shack at the bottom, the one with the broken roof and a cracked window.

I've been trying to reach him for days now, and it's unusual not to see him. He's always working or tending to something, always present, even if I can't approach him. But not recently; he's been hidden from me.

Perhaps he was sent away; Donovan had threatened that.

"All I have to do is mention him to my mother, and that bastard brother of mine you like so much will be gone. We could fetch a good price for him, too. A man who looks like him, young and virile."

As soon as he'd said it, my insides had coiled in dread, knowing that he would follow through just to spite me. I'm aware he hasn't because he would have gloated if Seth were gone, but I need to be sure.

When there is no answer to my soft knock on the door, I push it open gently and whisper his name into the darkness. "Seth..."

The air inside is cold, damp, and clammy, with a foul odour that stings my nostrils. I spot a candle on the window ledge and quickly light it.

"Oh, no...."

Seth is lying on the floor in front of the fire, wrapped in a blanket. I rush over to him. My heart aches, fearing the worst as I kneel beside him. He blinks, licks his lips., "Katherine...."

"Shush, don't try to speak." *I get up and hurry to the small jug, only to find it empty. I must fetch water from the stream, but I'm torn. Leaving him alone could be condemning him to death. But what choice do I have?*

I rush outside, jug in hand, fill it, and rush back. I pour water into a glass and offer it to him, holding it to his lips so he can drink.

It causes him to cough and wince. He pulls the blanket more tightly around himself, huddling down. "S-so c-cold."

"You have a fever." *I slowly pull the blanket down, revealing his back. It's covered in numerous slices and slashes. I bite my lip to stifle a trembling gasp.* "This is because of me."

He shakes his head slowly.

"Did Donovan have them do this?" *I demand, though I don't need an answer. I'm all too aware of his brother's cruelty. My own scars and bruises bear witness to it. Seth does not reply, and I gently brush his damp hair back.* "I'm going to light a fire and warm some water. Those wounds need cleaning."

"No," *he protests weakly.*

"Yes."

He reaches out to stop me ... or maybe push me away; it's hard to tell. Regardless, I grasp his hand firmly, my heart and body quivering with fear. I lower my head close to his. "I can't lose you," *I whisper shakily. He's the only light in my life, the only thing I have to hold onto, even if I never actually touch him. Just knowing he's there is enough.*

"I am here for you, always," he reassures me in a whisper.

"Then let me be here for you. You have an infection. These wounds need to be cleaned."

"They will find you here—"

"Then let them."

He tries to hold onto me, but I slip my hand away and go to the fireplace. It hasn't been lit in days, not even warm embers remain. The last time I saw Seth was when he sneaked me back into the main house, five days ago. That's how long there has been no fire, and the frost is creeping in, if only in the mornings for now. Soon, the grass will turn hard and frozen.

There are no berries left on the trees or bushes. We've preserved what we could into jams and pies, but there will be no more. The seasons are changing.

I start a new fire by clearing out the old ashes and debris. There's only a small pile of wood beside it, and Seth hasn't been able to chop more. Perhaps I can sneak some from the main house and bring it down later.

I use the bowl to boil the water over the fire, and it feels like it takes an eternity. Seth dozes in and out of consciousness, and I can't help but touch his face, pushing his hair back, letting my fingers linger on his skin. His complexion is unnaturally pale and ashen. Leaning closer to him, I murmur, "I'm so sorry."

"It's not your fault," he whispers and coughs, reaching for me,.

I gasp as I wake, the remnants of the dream clinging to me like a heavy cloak, suffusing me with fear and guilt. Seth's name is on my lips, but the bed is empty beside me. Moonlight filters in through the windows, and there's no trace that he was ever here, except for the indentation where his body once lay. A sense of coldness envelops me in his absence, and a profound feeling of loss settles in, though it doesn't make sense.

I place my hand on my chest, feeling my heart thumping against my ribs. I have to swallow hard to fight off a creeping sense of panic.

"Seth?" I call out, but I'm not sure if I'm referring to the Seth from my dream or the one I know. In my mind, they merge into one, as if my body recognises them both, even though they shouldn't be connected.

I sit up abruptly, and that's when I spot him standing in the corner of the room, watching me with gentle eyes. The deep blue of his dress shirt accentuates the pallor of his skin, making it almost luminescent in the moonlight. His hands are tucked into his pockets, but I can still feel the memory of how tightly they held mine just a few hours ago.

"I'm still here," Seth says softly as he takes a step closer to me.

I'm at a loss for words, my mind filled with these inexplicable stories and places that I shouldn't know, considering I had never met him until he bought me at the auction. Yet, my mind conjures up these narratives and memories that don't make any sense. It's as if there's more to my connection with him than I can comprehend. "You have scars on your back," I dare to say. "Your brother—"

"Had me lashed."

"Because of Katherine."

"Because of his blind heart. He had no true understanding of what he possessed."

CHAPTER
TWENTY-SEVEN

Seth's demeanour has shifted. The rest has revitalised him, and as he moves closer, there's an intensified strength, a more potent aura surrounding him.

"Did you see my dream?" I ask because I don't understand how he knows exactly what I'm talking about, nor does he question. His answer is so simple as if we'd been watching the same thing.

He gazes at me, a seemingly eternal moment passing between us. "These things you must learn on your own. It will come when the time is right. Everything happens when it's meant to." He steps closer, so near that I could reach out and touch him, and I find myself wanting, needing to. My body quivers with the urge.

The dream lingers in my mind, an ethereal whisper of memory, echoing Seth's essence. Emotions surge within me, a yearning to close the gap between us, to soothe the palpable concern radiating from him. In Seth, power and responsibility intertwine, each amplifying the other.

Katherine's emotions swirl through my thoughts like a haunting melody. Her yearning, her tender care for him, and the shadow of sorrow for her own fate are tangible. Amidst this emotional tapestry, there's an unmistakable thread of love—a love so pure and unique, it defies the understanding of their world.

"My mind feels impatient. I feel ..." My words trail off as I lock eyes with him. "About you. I feel ..."

His gaze is piercing. "Confused?"

I dislike the word 'confused.' It doesn't quite capture the complexity of my emotions.

His hand lowers to my cheek, his thumb lightly caressing my skin.

I feel myself drawn into him. "You're unlike any vampire I've ever met," I whisper. "I've been around your kind since childhood, but this ... it's indescribable. I should be afraid of you. But you're not like them," I find myself admitting, despite my reservations. Unlike Crevan and the others. 'You never take anything from me. Back at the compound, when I offered."

"You are not here for that."

When we had fallen, and Killian and his people had taken us back to their place. I offered to feed Seth. He had been injured, similar to how Layla was when we found her. Killian had wired Seth up for transfusions, a plan so well-executed it seemed premeditated. But Seth had needed to heal faster, and despite his weakened state, he had refused my offer to feed him, even when I almost forced him. The only reason he gave in was to save us.

"What am I here for?" I pause, piecing together this complex puzzle. "You walked in the sun because you fed from me? There is something with my blood?"

He closes his eyes briefly, as if fending off unwanted thoughts. "Yes," he admits, his thumb lightly caressing my lower lip, feather-light.

"What is it?"

He lowers his hand to mine, gently taking it and guiding me to stand with him. I have to tilt my head back to meet his gaze. Seth does what he always does, placing a finger under my chin to direct my face towards his. It's against my nature to maintain eye contact, trained as I am to look away, but with Seth, I find myself drawn to his eyes, to his face. My heart pounds, blood surging through my veins as our other hands remain entwined.

"I do not know exactly, but it calls to me, you call to me." Slowly, he lowers his face, his lips meeting mine with a gentleness I don't expect, warmer than I anticipate. A small gasp escapes my throat, a sound of surprise and awakening desire.

The warmth of his lips against mine sends a shock through my entire being. It's as if the world around us fades into nothingness, and all that exists in this moment is the intoxicating sensation of his touch. His lips are soft yet firm, moving against mine with a mesmerising rhythm that makes my head spin.

My heart races even faster, a wild flurry of emotions swirling within me. Desire blooms deep within my core, igniting a fire that I never knew existed. With each passing second, the boundaries between us blur, and I find myself losing control to this whirlwind of passion.

His hand tightens around mine, grounding me in reality as our bodies press closer together. The heat radiating from him seeps into my skin, warming every inch of me. In this embrace, time ceases to exist, and all that matters are the sensations coursing through my veins.

I melt into his touch, surrendering to the overwhelming desire. Every nerve ending comes alive under his gentle caress. It's a dance of tongues and sighs, an intricate symphony of shared breaths and tantalising kisses.

I float away, losing myself, as something in my mind opens—a spark, a door? I'm uncertain. A gasp escapes my lips.

"Show me where you are," demands a voice, thick, fluid, commanding and intrusive.

In my mind's eye, he appears as though standing before me—his handsome face, a physique exuding both command and deceit. His wicked grin sends chills through me, both pushing and pulling at my senses. He struggles to grasp my mind, toying with it.

"No," I resist, pushing back, fighting his intrusion.

"Show me, Payton. I will come for you," he insists.

Flashes, fragments of images:

Donova n.

"No, no... get away," I urge, seeing his hand reaching out to me. I scream, pushing with all my might to repel him. "No."

My eyes snap open, disoriented. I can't discern my location, my actions. Seth stands before me, but the embrace we shared is gone.

My breathing is ragged, each breath shallow and strained.

The door swings open. Killian stands there, his hair in disarray, his usual armour absent, replaced by loose-fitting pants, a blade in his hand. "I heard a scream. Is everything okay?" Sleep still weighs on his eyes, but his expression is alert.

Seth raises a hand, signalling Killian to keep his distance, then turns to me. "What happened?"

Looking at them both, I struggle to comprehend. Taking

a deep breath, I manage, "Donovan." The word hangs in the air. "I saw Donovan."

Killian's posture relaxes slightly, his blade lowering to rest beside his leg. "It was just a dream?"

Seth's intense gaze pierces me, as if he's delving into my soul. "No, that was no dream. He connected with you," he asserts, focusing on me, not Killian. "I felt his presence, too."

I nod. "He wanted to know where I was."

Seth inhales sharply, a mix of concern and urgency in his breath. "He's searching for her."

Killian steps into the room. "Maybe he's already found her?"

CHAPTER
TWENTY-EIGHT

"Damn, fucking bitch." Donovan erupts from his chair with such force that it goes sailing across the room, propelled by the fury of his temper. He rubs at his temples, feeling a pressure akin to a headache, an unfamiliar sensation he hasn't experienced in centuries.

Marcus lounges on a sofa, legs spread wide, arm stretched along the back, the very picture of a spoilt, rich kid. His curly dark hair cascades to his shoulders, his shirt casually unbuttoned. He watches Donovan's outburst with a mix of amusement and interest. "No joy?" he asks, almost tauntingly.

"No joy? She's locked down fucking tighter than a virgin on her wedding night," Donovan snaps, his hands slamming down onto the table. "I almost had her, almost saw into the room she's hidden in, but damn, he's got her stashed away securely."

Pacing the room, Donovan's mind races with strategies to reach her. They had this inkling, a faint hope, that since he'd once connected to her remotely at Seth's place, he might be able to do so again. He had tried, and by some stroke of luck, established a fragile link. However, penetrating her thoughts felt like wading through thick weeds in water—arduous and sluggish. Maybe it was the distance.

"Did you get anything out of the kid?" That's Amelia, posed on her own sofa. Unlike Marcus, she doesn't slouch. Amelia never slouches. She sits with elegance, legs together, her body poised in a picture of perfection. Her hands rest on her knees, her long, painted nails rhythmically drumming.

"Do you have to do that in here?" Donovan's voice cuts through the room, his irritation directed at Marcus. In his relaxed state, Marcus has company—a slim, small woman draped across the sofa beside him. Her legs rest on him, one drawn up to his chest, where his fingers trace her inner thigh. Blood, evidence of his recent feeding, pools around the bite mark, and she lies there, her head tilted back in ecstasy, seemingly oblivious to her near-nakedness, clad only in a flimsy string barely covering her.

Her small breasts occasionally draw Marcus's attention as he feeds, enhancing the pleasure for both. The woman's expression is one of bliss, lost in another world entirely.

"You wanted me here for this, and I'm in the middle of dinner," Marcus responds nonchalantly, unbothered by Donovan's disapproval.

Amelia, witnessing the scene, rolls her eyes and stands up. "The boy doesn't know anything, or he's refusing to tell us," she reports, her attention shifting away from the spectacle. Examining her fingers, she notices blood on the underside of her arm—Nico's blood. He's become her toy, a plaything in her dangerous games.

Donovan drums his fingers, glaring at his two vampire companions with a mix of tolerance and suspicion. They are allies, yet the trust between them is as tenuous as it is mutual. He taps his finger impatiently on the desk. "I'm going to interrogate him myself again. Let's see what the little shit knows."

"I doubt you'll extract much from him," Amelia retorts, a grin spreading across her lips. Her lips are a vivid red, not from lipstick but from something far more visceral. Her eyes, too, seem to mirror this crimson hue, as if infused with blood.

Shaking his head in disdain, Donovan remarks, "You'd think you'd both be beyond playing with your food by now." His gaze shifts to the woman with Marcus, noticing her own hand wandering beneath her scant garment. "Does she really have to do that here?"

Not waiting for a response, nor expecting one, Donovan exits the room, a fiery rage coursing through his veins, fuelling him like lava. He strides toward the basement door, his presence causing humans to step aside. Jonathan's people, pathetic as they are, still part for him. One gets too close, earning a snarl from Donovan, but even this doesn't deter a woman at the reception desk from smiling at him flirtatiously. Perhaps one day he'll show her exactly what she's flirting with.

The security team, a mix of humans and vampires, stands guard at the door. Donovan yanks it open with such force it nearly rips from its hinges and storms down the steps.

The basement is dark and damp, the stench overpowering even to his heightened senses. Though his vampiric nature sometimes dulls certain perceptions, smells like these remain acutely unpleasant.

"Open the damn gate," Donovan commands. The human seated at the desk, watching, scrambles to comply.

He pulls the keys from his pocket, mumbling a hasty "Yes, sir," while fumbling, nearly dropping them. However, he manages to fit the key into the lock and opens it.

Nico remains motionless inside, curled up on his side with his eyes closed.

"Get up," Donovan demands, but Nico doesn't stir.

He's naked, his skin pallid, marked by claw marks that Donovan is certain are Amelia's handiwork. "I said, get up," he repeats, his voice rising in frustration.

Still, Nico remains unmoved. "I know you're not dead. I can feel your heart beating," Donovan says, noting that the rhythm isn't fast but rather slow and erratic, not the pattern of someone sleeping.

"Ameilia ..." Donovan exhales in exasperation. She's pushed the boy to the brink of death, interpreting Donovan's command of not killing him in her own twisted way. Nico is dangerously close to death.

Donovan leans in, turning Nico over. The boy's eyes are hooded, barely open, his lips cracked, eyes bloodshot to an almost vampiric red, his skin a sickly grey. "You humans are so weak, so pathetic. I'm glad I only spent twenty-nine years as one," Donovan sneers, his lip curling with disdain. "You don't deserve what I'm about to give you."

Anger courses through Donovan, fueling a transformation. It's like a magic within him, and he harnesses it, feeling it spread through his body. His fingers begin to change shape, nails retracting as claws emerge.

Nico's eyes suddenly widen, watching Donovan transform. He shakes his head, trying to recoil.

Donovan grabs him, his features now more beast than man or vampire, with sharp, canine-like teeth. He leans in close to Nico. "This will make you all better," he whispers menacingly, then bites.

CHAPTER
TWENTY-NINE

My chest feels tight, and my breathing becomes erratic. Donovan's face keeps appearing in my mind. It's not just an image or a memory; it's as if he's actually inside my head.

It's what their kind does. "How could he reach me like this? Doesn't he have to be close to do that?" Realisation dawns, and my eyes widen. "Does this mean he's here?"

I stagger back, not to distance myself from Seth, but from the possibility that his brother …

"He's not here," Seth assures me, his gaze intense. "If he were, we'd know. I think my brother is desperate. That's all this is. He's connected with you before, so he can do it again. Could Craven connect when he wasn't close?"

"Not with me." My voice drops. "Craven barely bothered with me. My blood seemed to repel him. He only tried it when desperate, saying it made him ill. But he never refused the sex. Fortunately, his aversion meant he didn't summon me often. I was just a toy he thought he wanted, not what he actually needed. That's why we never had a connection."

"But with others?"

"Yes," I confirm. "He connected with others, and I've witnessed it. Our minds are never safe."

"Your minds are like locked doors. Once we find the key, we can always open them," Seth says.

"So he used that door to try and find me."

"Yes, and he failed."

"I pushed him out," I say, a sense of pride in my voice.

Seth tilts his head. "You pushed him out?"

I nod. "I told him 'no'. I pushed back and slammed the mental doors shut. He was furious. I felt this sudden burst of anger as he left."

"My brother doesn't like to be told 'no', whatever the occasion. I've never known a human who can push us out of their minds, but then ..." Seth pauses, placing his hand gently on my face, studying me. "I've never met a human like you before, either." He holds my gaze for what feels like a long minute. "I need to check the lands around this place. Naneve mentioned we might have some unwelcome visitors lurking. I don't think my brother will try again, at least not tonight. I brought you some clothing; Elena got them for you. She wasn't sure about your size and had to guess. Anything you don't like, you can change. I'm afraid your old clothes were torn and tattered, as were ours."

My clothes were, our clothes were ... maybe Seth's the worst. It doesn't matter. Theo had given me something to sleep in, and I'd not worried beyond that. Clothing was a luxury in Craven's place, so it never entered my head to think about it.

There are clothes at the end of my bed. I reach for them; they're soft. "Thank you," I say. "What time is it?" I realise I've lost track of time, the days and hours just flying by in a blur of events.

"A little after eleven," he answers. "There's a bathroom through that door," he gestures. "Shower, dress, and come down. Theo is preparing a hot meal. You must be hungry."

His mention of food suddenly makes me realise my hunger, because yes, I am. Even with everything. "Yes."

He doesn't step back from me immediately. Instead, he tilts my head up and places his lips to mine, inhaling deeply. He closes his eyes, as if savouring the touch. It makes me swallow hard, wanting to reach out to him. Then he moves his face, sliding until we're cheek to cheek, his mouth near my ear. "Katherine."

He pulls back and, without another word, heads towards the door. "Come down when you're ready." And then he's gone, leaving me to sigh deeply.

The feel of his lips against mine lingers like a faint whisper. My heart tightens as I watch him leave and listen to his footsteps fade away.

"Katherine," I whisper her name. The sound of it on his lips does something to me, and I don't know what.

Seth and Katherine. A woman with whom I could never compete.

CHAPTER
THIRTY

I opt for the solitude of my room, leaving his behind. The dying embers in the hearth still provide a muted warmth, their dim glow creating a cosy atmosphere. The curtains are wide open, showcasing a star-filled sky and trees coated in sparkling frost. The scene outside reminds me of childhood walks on similar frosty grounds, the crunching sound underfoot bringing a sense of nostalgia.

The world now endures erratic weather patterns, with blistering days swiftly turning into freezing nights, a testament to the environmental damage caused by human activities. Such unpredictability has become the norm.

There's a belief, I don't know where from, that vampires emerged as a necessity for our survival, their transformation into immortality being a means to endure. This idea seems plausible, considering our enhanced strength.

Others claim that vampires were created by witches.

I open a previously unexplored door in my room. To my surprise, it's a shared bathroom with two entrances, one from my room and the other from Seth's, reminiscent of the bathroom in Skin Trade. I wonder if this arrangement is intentional on his part or just a coincidence.

The bathroom itself is spacious, dominated by a clawfooted bathtub at its heart. My feelings are ambivalent; it's grand and spectacular, but it's also a place of pain in my mind. Not this particular bath, but the ones the vampires used in their attempts to cleanse our bodies of the virus that claimed so many lives.

I push those thoughts aside and take a refreshing shower. The water is hot and steaming, just as I had hoped. The soap is delicately scented and gentle on my skin and I let my thoughts drift to Seth and the way he kissed me.

He kissed me ...

Once I'm clean, dry, and dressed, I stand in front of the mirror. The glass is misted with condensation, and I wipe it with my hand. As I study my reflection, I struggle to recognise myself. I lean in close, bracing my hands on the counter, and stare at my long blonde hair framing my face. It seems thinner than I remember, and my eyes appear darker.

During my time at Crevan's, mirrors were a necessity. We had to apply makeup, style our hair, and present ourselves as attractive commodities for the vampires' parties and gatherings. Nobody wants a miserable and dull-looking "meal," so we were compelled to dress up, apply makeup, and smell appealing, though perfume on our skin was unnecessary—vampires had no use for it when biting into our necks, thighs, and other preferred areas.

Exiting the bathroom and my room, I retrace Theo's path that led me here when he showed me to the bedroom. I hope I'm heading in the right direction. The place is grand, with wood-lined corridors adorned with paintings, furniture, sofas, tables, and chairs. There are sculptures, statues, and intricate wall lights.

Eventually, I reach the staircase we ascended. At the time, I was so exhausted and confused that I didn't fully absorb my surroundings. Now, I carefully descend the stairs, my hand sliding along the thick bannister. At the bottom, I hear voices growing louder, confirming I'm on the right path.

I cross the hallway to a large, thick wooden door and gently push it open. It's the kitchen, and it feels like the central hub of the house. The layout reminds me of Seth's shack in my dreams, with similar wooden panels, an old table, antiques, and numerous books on the shelves.

Several faces turn to look at me as I enter the room, but it is only one that most surprises me to see.

Layla.

She is sitting at the table. Her brightly coloured hair now appears dull and is pulled back from her face. She no longer exudes the vibrant vigour she once did, resembling a discarded and forgotten plaything left aside for many years.

Naneve is also seated at the table, eating porridge from a bowl. She takes a bite of the apple she is holding as her eyes lock onto me. Theo stands over the stove, focused on the pan in which he is cooking more porridge. Killian and Seth are not back yet.

"Come, sit," Theo says, gesturing towards a vacant seat opposite Naneve as he places a steaming bowl on the table for me. He carries the pan over and ladles its contents into my bowl. "If you're extra hungry, we've got fresh fruit—bananas, apples, and some strawberries. They're out of season, so they're not the best, but still good. And we have nuts and seeds, too, if you'd like," he adds, placing a spoon beside the bowl.

"Thank you," I say, my senses awakening to the hot, sweet aroma of the food. I reach for a banana, my usual apprehension under Naneve's sharp gaze momentarily forgotten. Ordinarily, I'd be shrinking under her scrutinising stare, trying to interpret what I've always perceived as her unkind, critical thoughts about me. Her disdain has never been a secret. But today, my focus drifts towards Layla over the chair that separates us.

Layla sits motionless, save for her eyes, which track my every move with an unsettling intensity. Her hands lie on the table, but her fingers move slowly, almost hypnotically, as she lightly scratches a pattern on the wooden surface.

I can't help but ask, "Are you okay?"

Layla's gaze lifts to mine, her head stiff. Her eyes, once filled with gentleness, now burn red with bright, unsettling edges. The warmth that once resided there has vanished, replaced by a fierce, unnerving hunger. I shift in my seat, uncomfortably aware of her predatory stare—it's like standing near the thirsty, feeling their hunger as a palpable force.

Her right hand presses deeper into the wooden table, splintering the surface under her relentless fingers. Theo, having ceased cooking, joins me in watching her with growing concern. We all seem to be holding our breath in unison.

"Layla ...." Theo's voice is a soft murmur.

"Is she okay now?" I ask, my mind racing back to the last time I saw her, far from this frightening state. Her gaze, once glassy, is now clear but menacing.

Her upper lip twitches, revealing elongated fangs—a sign of a vampire's true nature. Seth can conceal his, so Layla's display is a deliberate act of aggression.

"I think I should return to my room," I suggest tentatively. Before this turns into something more. I don't like what I feel coming off her. It's dark and hungry.

Theo's hand presses down on my shoulder, his grip protective. "I don't think it's wise to move," he whispers.

Naneve stops eating and her hand drifts to her blade, ready for whatever may come. The room is thick with tension, a mix of desire and desperation.

"Please, don't," I whisper to Layla, my breath uneven. She's like a coiled spring, and I feel like prey in her presence.

Layla leans forward, her voice trembling, "I can smell your blood. I-I can ..."

Naneve's blade is half-drawn, ready for action. The atmosphere is electric with potential violence.

The door swings open, and Seth enters with a commanding presence. His gaze sweeps over each of us—Layla, Theo, Naneve, and me—assessing the situation and the tension that grips the room. There's an almost tangible aura of power that seems to radiate from him as he moves.

"Layla, my love," he says, his voice deep and resonant.

But she doesn't seem to be listening. The snarl emanating from her grows louder, a rumbling sound from her chest. I slowly rise from my seat, and this time, Theo lets me. His hand, though, remains protectively on my shoulder. Naneve stands as well, her blade raised.

Layla hisses and, in a flash, lunges, her chair tumbling backwards as she lurches forward across the table in an attempt to reach me.

Theo grabs me and twists so that his body shields me. Layla's claws dig into Theo's back and she lets out an unholy shriek.

Theo's face contorts in pain, and Naneve leaps forward, her sword flashing.

Layla dodges it easily.

"Layla." Seths' stern voice commands attention, redirecting the prevailing power in the room.

Layla's head whips around and her gaze fixes on her master's intense stare. "It's time for you to calm down." His command is firm, brooking no disobedience.

My heart is pounding in my chest as I take in the scene before me. Layla is panting heavily, her rage seemingly quelled by Seth's presence. However, I can still sense the danger simmering beneath the surface, a pressure building like a storm ready to erupt at any moment.

Theo groans behind me, but my attention stays focused on Seth and Layla, who are now engaged in an intense, silent standoff, their eyes locked like two adversaries on the brink of battle.

"*Enough*," says Seth.

CHAPTER
THIRTY-ONE

Layla slumps at Seth's feet, her previously menacing demeanour vanishing. She collapses weakly to the floor. Bloody tears trickle from her eyes, and she uses the back of her hand to wipe them away, smearing her face in red across her pale skin. Her voice, almost inaudible but laden with sobs, pleads with him. Her face twists into a tortured expression when she finally speaks again.

"I'm sorry .... I'm so sorry ...."

Abruptly, she switches to a different language, to which Seth responds in kind. He takes a breath, and his words come out slowly, as if he has vocalised them a thousand times before. "Go and sit on the chair. Do not move unless I order it."

"Yes, sir." She scrambles to the chair on her hands and knees without looking at me. When she is seated, she turns away from me, avoiding my stare.

My attention is soon diverted by a sound behind me. I spin around, dropping to my knees in front of a wounded Theo.

"Oh, God," he groans. The sweat on his forehead gathers into tiny beads, and blood stains the floor around him like a red halo. "My pills," he rasps, extending a shaky finger to point behind me. "Get my pills .... The red ones."

I quickly turn to locate the cabinet he's pointing at and then proceed to open its door.

"What the hell just happened?" Naneve demands. "What the hell was that? Is she a problem?"

Seth redirects his gaze to meet Naneve's, and the intensity of his look could compel even me to back down. He glares at her.

She lowers her tone and rephrases her question. "What was that? What did she just do?"

"She is okay," Seth grounds out, then moves across the room to Theo and kneels beside him. "Can you sit up?"

Theo grits his teeth and nods.

"Is she a danger to us?" Naneve continues her questions. "Do we need to lock her up? Because it's bad enough we're confined here, and everyone is still at the compound. It's bad enough we're hiding."

Seth's jaw tightens. "We are not hiding."

"No?" She moves around the table to stand over Seth as he helps Theo remove his cardigan. "Then what is this? We're behind locked walls, in a place no one knows, protected by witch wards. If that isn't hiding—"

Seth gets up abruptly, and Naneve cowers back. "Are we having a problem here?"

She clenches her jaw but says nothing.

"I didn't think so. Go and get Killian. He's in the back garden pulling out the quads. Elena is with Tasha. Bring them here, then I suggest you take some rest yourself."

"I'm not tired. I don't need to rest."

"I wasn't offering a suggestion." Seth dismisses her, returning to Theo, and Naneve is left standing there, glaring at the back of his head. Then she looks at me, and I can sense she wants to speak, or yell, and perhaps lay the blame not just on Layla but on me for all of it, whatever "it" may be.

"I hope you're right about her, or we're all screwed," she says before leaving.

I retrieve the pills from the cabinet, although I'm uncertain which ones he wants. Three bottles stand proudly on the shelf, all red, with three different shades and none of them labelled. But that's the norm now, and it has been for a long time.

Basic medications, such as aspirin and ibuprofen, became as scarce as illegal drugs in the first few days after the virus struck. With pharmacies ransacked, most people had no choice but to look for makeshift remedies.

I remember the first pharmacy near my home being attacked about a month after the chaos began. An angry mob stormed through the door, grabbing every tablet, capsule, or bottle they could find—every drop of alcohol-based lotion was snatched with a grimy hand. Once everything of value was taken up, the thugs turned on the store owner, Mr. Patel. He was killed during the raid while his wife was injured. She remained hidden in the back room until it was safe to come out again. By daybreak, all that remained were empty shelves and rows of shattered mirrors reflecting broken glass, and blood staining splintered wood floors.

People got creative, mixing medications with creams and ointments. Some were deadly, and some weren't. Yet, the overall effect remained the same: basic medication became a rarity, and the only way to obtain even a paracetamol was through the black market.

I take the three bottles over to Theo, and Seth looks at me. "Help me get his shirt off."

Setting the medicine on the table, I crouch next to him. As I do, the door opens, and Elena and Killian enter, almost competing to squeeze through the door simultaneously.

"What the hell happened?" Killian asks, though his tone is not as accusatory as Naneve's earlier.

Elena's eyes grow wide. "Oh, God, Theo—"

He raises his hand to fend her off. "I'm okay. It's just a scratch."

Killian peers down at him. "That doesn't look like a scratch to me."

Between Seth and me, we lift Theo's shirt. The fibres seem to have completely meshed with his wound. "Is it fusing with his skin?" I ask. It appears as if the fabric is healing inside; the white threads weave in and out of the pink flesh. "Yes," Seth replies while carefully peeling the shirt upward. I assist him, pulling it over Theo's shoulders and then the undershirt beneath.

How many layers does one man need?

The clothes are ruined, shredded where Layla's claws tore through.

"This is going to need stitches," Killian remarks, eyeing the wound.

"What were you doing?" Elena asks. "How on earth did this happen?"

Her question brings another sob from Layla, and guilt from me when I glance at her. "It wasn't her fault. Something happened when I came in, and she couldn't control it." I look at Seth. "She tried." I don't want him to punish her. "Theo tried to protect me. I-I could feel her hunger." I place a hand on my chest. "I could feel it here. It wasn't just hunger. It was more—it was a *need*."

"Like the thirsty," Killian murmurs.

I nod. "It's like ... I'm *connected* to them."

CHAPTER
THIRTY-TWO

Layla sits on the chair where Seth directed her, sobbing quietly. The sound unsettles me. I've always associated crying with not just mental anguish, but physical pain too—cruel, unpreventable pain.

It sends shivers through me, stirring memories I'd rather forget.

Compelled by an instinct I'm unsure of, I approach her. Maybe I shouldn't, maybe my presence alone causes her distress, but no one else is attending to her. Elena is preoccupied with Theo, while Seth and Killian are wrapped up in their own concerns, and, of course, in each other.

"Layla ..." I start, reaching out to touch her shoulder, to turn her to face me.

"Don't," she pleads. "Please ..." Her eyes, red and bloodshot, meet mine, revealing her inner turmoil. She's a mere shadow of the vibrant woman I met on that first night. We seem to have switched places—I see in her the same shock, weariness, and fear that I felt when I first entered the skin trade, lost and frightened in an alien world.

"I'm sorry," I whisper.

She shakes her head, pushing me away, yet her hands slide down to mine. Unintentionally, our fingers intertwine. My perception shifts, the real world blurring as my mind takes over. I take a deep breath, trying to anchor myself, battling the onslaught of emotions.

It's cold, dark, and the relentless rain hasn't ceased for days. Hunger and exhaustion aren't my feelings; they're Layla's, experienced indirectly. "Layla ..." I repeat.

It's as if I'm standing right beside her, able to touch her essence.

She's curled up on the wet ground, wrapped in a coat, shivering. Her eyes are shut tight, lips tinged an eerie shade of blue. The air reeks of fresh blood—hers. Leaning against a bin, she uses it for shelter from the rain and support for her weary body.

A man enters the alley, pausing at its entrance, hands in pockets. He looks around as if checking for observers before disappearing into the shadows.

As he towers over her, her eyes widen with fear. She shakes her head, blood streaking down her face, diluted by the rain into her jacket. Her once-bright hair is matted with blood.

She clutches the side of her neck, blood oozing from the wound. The man—Seth, inhales sharply, drawn here by the scent of blood. His fangs are exposed, yet he isn't biting her; he's observing.

"Please ..." her voice is a weak plea.

I see more of her story unfold like pieces of a puzzle. Her coat falls open, revealing the little she wears underneath and her body, marked with bruises. The blood from her neck has trickled down, staining her skin. The bruises on her thighs speak volumes of her ordeal.

She struggles to swallow, to breathe. Each deep breath she takes seems to exact a toll. "Please ... kill me ..."

Seth's vampire precision is evident as he gently takes her hand from her neck. Each movement he makes is deliberate, calculated. He examines the wound on her throat; the skin is torn, the muscles visible as if someone has savagely tried to rip it out.

She coughs, her eyes rolling back, and more blood spurts out. Seth crouches beside her, his hand not to feed but to help, yet the potential for more is there.

"I can save you," he says. "I can make it all better."

Her eyes meet his, filled with a profound desperation. She weakly lifts her hand.

"Do you want me to?"

"Help me ..." she begs. "Please ..."

Seth rolls up the sleeve of his arm, as I saw him do within the glass case.

His silver, blade-like fangs glint in the dim light as he bites into his own wrist with fierce determination. Blood wells up, a vibrant crimson, seeping from the wound. He extends his bleeding arm towards her, offering his own blood as a means of salvation.

Her eyes widen, a tumult of fear and desperate hope swirling within them. She trembles as she reaches towards Seth's wrist, her fingers hesitating above the throbbing vein. The scent of her blood fills the air, mingling with the damp earthiness of the rain-soaked alley.

"Drink," he whispers, his voice a soft, haunting melody resonating through her broken spirit. "Take my blood, be reborn."

She hesitates, uncertainty shadowing her delicate features. The burden of her suffering weighs heavily upon her, threatening the fragile ember of life flickering within.

Yet, in a moment of introspection, a spark of resilience kindles within her.

With a resolve born of desperation, she clasps Seth's wrist with both hands, bringing it to her lips. Her tongue tentatively meets the wound, tasting the metallic richness of his blood before she drinks eagerly. The elixir floods her mouth, a bittersweet nectar, overwhelming her senses. Seth's life force surges through her, igniting her skin with an electrifying warmth.

As she drinks, the world around her fades into a hazy abyss. Time loses its hold, replaced by an intense rush of sensations, memories, and desires swirling in her mind.

I feel the transformation as if it were my own; Seth's blood is altering her.

He watches, a complex mix of anticipation and concern on his face. A subtle transformation unfolds within her, her pallid complexion gaining a rosy flush, a newfound vitality emanating from her being.

But as certain as I can reach for a discarded bottle on the ground, I can reach for her life, for the golden glow streaming from him to her. All it takes is a pull, and she'd be gone.

Jolted back to reality, I release Layla's hand. She recoils as if burnt by my touch.

"I saw ..." I stammer, looking between Seth and her. "I saw when you turned her. She was in an alleyway, attacked, dying. And you ... you saved her."

"She was dying," Seth says, his gaze going from me to her and back again. "Dying, and I offered her a new life, so she accepted." His gaze shifts to me. "But how do you know this?"

I glance at Layla, now no longer crying but looking at

me with an expression mirroring the others' wonder. "Because I saw it," I say. "I saw her, and I saw you."

CHAPTER
THIRTY-THREE

Theo sits astride a chair, its back pressed to his chest, as Elena meticulously cleans the fibres from his wound. She works with painstaking care, extracting each fibre from his skin to aid healing. The wound is a vivid red, appearing more aggravated than healing in my eyes. It looks sore, the kind that would make me wince and turn away.

Despite Theo's injury, the attention in the room has shifted. I've inadvertently become the focus. Theo, Elena, and even Killian, who clenches something so tightly in his hand that his knuckles have turned white. A tic pulses along his jawline.

"She isn't human, is she?" Killian asks, his voice lacking malice but filled with confusion. "She something entirely different?"

I turn to Seth, seeking answers to the same question. Before all this, if someone had claimed I wasn't human, I would have internally refuted it, denied any extraordinary power. But now, unless I'm lost in an incredibly vivid dream, I'm uncertain.

I am me, the ordinary version in a world where everything I thought I knew has been upended. So, why not question what I know about myself?

Seth returns my gaze, his intense stare as if he can see right through me. "I don't know," he admits.

"But you know something?" Killian presses, his question heavy with significance, echoing my own desperate need for understanding.

I don't divulge the golden thread I sensed, a thread I'm sure I could pull to end her existence. It's a feeling so right yet unexplainable, like an innate knowledge without understanding.

As a child, I often felt out of place, harbouring a sense of strangeness within. It was why I struggled to make friends, why they labelled me 'weird' and other terms I prefer not to recall. But this feeling is different, more like a fiery energy pulsing through my veins.

"I am human," I assert firmly. "Both my parents are human."

Killian shakes his head, a gesture not of disbelief, but contemplation. "That may be so, but everything that's happening ..." He steps back, hand outstretched as if to emphasise his point. "This is not typical human behaviour." He pauses, observing me thoughtfully. "You survived the virus when no one else on the planet did. How? How can you be human and do that?"

"But you never got it at all, did you?" I counter.

His tone isn't angry; it's curious, a pursuit for understanding. If there were anger, maybe Seth would intervene. "I am immune, but there are many of us. You are the only person I've heard of who contracted it and lived."

He's sincere; everyone knows no one survives Alitora.

The news was clear about it. When I got it, I felt my body fighting it off, resisting its invasion.

Theo frowns in disbelief. "She got sick and lived?"

Killian nods affirmatively. "Yes." He turns back to Seth. "Is there something in her blood? She survived the virus, the thirsty are drawn to her, Layla is drawn to her, and then …" The unspoken implications hang in the air, almost tangible.

"Seth walked in sunlight after drinking from me?" I add, throwing in my own piece of the puzzle.

"Exactly," Killian confirms. "You enabled him to walk in sunlight after he drank from you. How? What's causing all this?"

Even Elena, who had been tending to Theo, is now watching us intently. They're unfamiliar with these occurrences. "That's what I sense about you," she remarks, stepping closer but maintaining a respectful distance. She studies me, her gaze lingering just above my head. "It's like energy radiating from you." She looks towards Seth. "Couldn't we test her blood? Take her to St Mary's. They still have their facilities. I could use it. I could--"

Seth's objection is immediate and firm. "No."

Elena's eyes dart to Seth, clearly shocked at the harshness of his reply. "But why not? We need to know what's going on. This could help us."

Killian nods in agreement, his brow furrowed with confusion. He looks from Elena to Seth and back again, his eyes searching for answers. The room is heavy with tension, the air charged as if a storm is about to break. Leaning against the wall, Seth crosses his arms over his chest, making a visible effort to control his emotions. "There's too much at stake," he finally explains. "She is too important."

Elena frowns, her nose twitching as she inhales deeply.

"I understand that, but if she can help us understand what's happening with Layla—and the others like her—then we need to take advantage of it." She reaches out and places a gentle hand on my arm. Her skin is cool to the touch, her fingers soft like silk as they brush against my shirt sleeve. There's a spark between us, a connection that resonates deep within me. Elena leans closer, examining my face with piercing eyes that seem to see right through me. "I've never seen anything like you," she murmurs softly, tilting her head to the side in curiosity. "You're not just special, you're ... magical."

Killian nods, his gaze settling on me thoughtfully. "Elena has a point," he says, weighing his words. "If we uncover why she survived Alitora and why she attracts vampires... it could be a game-changer."

Seth exhales sharply, his frustration evident. He paces the room, each step resonating against the hardwood floor, amplifying the tension in the silent space. "And what if we discover it's nothing? What if we endanger her for mere curiosity?"

Elena, ever practical, suggests, "What if we went in daylight? Nothing could get to her then. The few thirsty we have in the area will be in hiding. Any at St Mary's can be dealt with easily."

Seth's shoulders tense, his usual calm

CHAPTER
THIRTY-FOUR

The pain inside him is unlike anything he's ever experienced. It's a searing, consuming fire, tearing through every vein with teeth and claws. This agony reaches down to his very core, prying apart the fibres of every bone in his body.

Nico clenches his jaw, grinding his teeth in a futile attempt to draw in breath, but nothing eases his torment.

He's sprawled on the floor of the grand room, an object of Donovan's twisted satisfaction. "I want to watch," Donovan had declared, his eyes fixated on Nico as he writhed in agony, his body convulsing uncontrollably.

Nico tries to speak, to beg. '*Please help me,*' is what he wants to say. '*Please kill me,*' is what he thinks.

Sweat beads down his face and throat, coating his back in a greasy sheen.

Inside, his body undergoes a monstrous transformation, birthing a creature unique and wild. Every cell reshapes and reimagines itself, adopting new structure and purpose. The lycanthrope virus courses through him, commanding every blood cell to die and be reborn into something more formidable.

Donovan senses it too, like a sorrowful melody strumming against his heartstrings. But instead of misery, it brings him a perverse sense of peace.

Nico is reduced to a weeping, helpless form on the floor at their feet.

Amelia stands over him, hands on her hips, her face twisted in disdain. There's no trace of guilt or remorse, no shred of empathy for what the boy endures. Her humanity, with all its accompanying emotions, is a distant memory. "Did you really have to do this to him?" she challenges Donovan, who is absorbed in studying a large map on the table, his hands braced against it.

Donovan's response is a noncommittal grunt.

Frustrated, Amelia approaches him. "I liked him. He tasted good. Now you've ruined him."

Donovan finally looks up at her like a father looking at an irritating child. "We'll find you a new toy."

"But I liked that one," she says, revealing a glimpse of her twisted attachment.

Donovan casts a glance at Nico. Huddled on his side, Nico quivers, his naked body exposed and unattended. There's no point in clothing him now. As the transformation ravages his body, any fabric would simply tear under the strain. Along his spine, a striking line of fur emerges, signalling his rapid metamorphosis. His once gentle facial features twist and harden, heralding a more primal form. A piercing scream erupts from him as new, larger canines brutally displace his human teeth.

Donovan, recalling the searing pain of his own transformation, can't help but savour the memory, especially the shock on Seth's face at his transformation.

Facing Amelia's earlier complaint, Donovan dismisses her with a nonchalant shrug. "He was mine first. I've just taken him back."

Donovan coldly turns away from Nico's torment, focusing instead on the maps in front of him. He only momentarily pauses when Nico's agonised screams pierce the air. Nico's involuntary bodily responses barely register to Donovan. By Donovan's count, Nico has already lost control of his body twice. He decides against cleaning him up now; there's no point in it yet.

Once the transformation completes, the remnants of Nico's humanity will be nothing more than blood, urine, and faeces on the floor.

The sharp rap at the door interrupts the scene. Blake, Donovan's vampire servant, opens it to find Amy standing there. Amy, one of Donovan's vampires. Her short black hair sharply contrasts with her bright blue eyes, the latter accentuated by the crimson residue of her recent feeding.

Donovan's attention shifts as Amelia, clad in a silk gown and perfectly tailored shoes, contrasts sharply with Amy's attire of combat pants, boots, and a jacket. Amy's long black leather coat seems almost too heavy for her slight frame. "Do you have news of my brother?" Donovan inquires, his standard query for any of his team.

They're a competent group: loyal and hardworking, albeit not the brightest, which is precisely why he leads them.

Amy unceremoniously drops a bag on the table and opens it. "That's all that was left in the vault," she announces.

Donovan delves into the bag, finding little of interest. It's filled with pictures, trinkets, and jewellery. He extracts a necklace draped over a silk box, letting it dangle from his fingers. The clear-cut diamond set in the necklace catches the light from the chandelier, casting prismatic colours across his face. "You can have this," he offers, extending it towards Amelia with a tilted smile. "Consider it an apology."

The stone in the necklace is cut into a teardrop shape. Amelia takes it, holding it in her palm to examine it more closely. The stones within sparkle intensely. "It doesn't completely make up for it, but it's a start," she remarks.

Donovan nods, then turns his attention to Amy. "Any progress?"

Amy sighs, shaking her head. "Sadly, no, sir. We found two of his men hiding in the back. One, a bar worker, claims ignorance. The other, a former aide of Seth's, is proving more interesting but equally unforthcoming," she reports with a snort. "I've sent them both to the camp for processing along with the others. They'll probably talk soon enough under Regan's methods."

"And Lucius?" Donovan asks.

Amy shakes her head again. "Nothing on him yet. But the aide will know something, I'm sure."

"There you go, Amelia," Donovan says with a hint of satisfaction. "I've got you a new toy to play with already."

"You're delegating the dirty work to me?" Amelia says. "Getting the information, you can't?"

"I'm assigning you a task you excel in. Do you want it, or should I send in Marcus?"

Her wicked grin says it all. "I'll do it. Do you want him alive?"

Donovan pauses, then shrugs nonchalantly. "It's not important."

"You're such a narcissist, Donovan Hayden," Amelia almost purrs.

"And that's precisely why you're here. Now go. Play. Have some fun. Show our other guests at the camp what happens if they don't start cooperating with me. And in the meantime, find out what that useless human is doing."

"I saw Jonathon on my way in. He's got some kind of meeting."

Amelia hasn't gone yet. She's at Nico again. "I don't know why you keep that fool around. If you just ended him …"

"It's more fun this way."

CHAPTER
THIRTY-FIVE

The night stretches on endlessly, each minute lingering longer than the last. I sit on the floor in the lounge, keeping the fire lit. Elena taught me the art of fire-making, a task less daunting than I expected. With a supply of kindling at my side, I feed the flames, maintaining their comforting warmth. The fire's glow brings back memories of Christmas trips with my parents to a cabin in the Lake District, a time when the world was untouched by current turmoil.

Back then, we imagined this decade would bring advancements. For some, it has, but humanity faces a starkly different reality—a world battered and bruised.

In that cabin, we had a coal fire. My mother and I would lug in sacks of coal. We'd curl up in front of it, the TV's flickering light dancing across our faces as we sang along to familiar tunes. Those memories are bittersweet; my mother's absence leaves a void, and thoughts of my father stir emotions I'm not ready to confront.

Elena keeps me occupied, guiding me through the process of grinding herbs, meticulously filling small bags and jars. Each one gets a label and a precise weighing. She's in the kitchen, engaged in a concoction of her own, something beyond ordinary cuisine. Tasha lounges on the sofa, her hand rhythmically moving over a pad, the strokes suggesting she's sketching rather than writing.

Elena has chosen to keep Layla separate from me, perhaps intentionally. Our glances inadvertently meet, reigniting the haunting memory of that alley scene—Layla's transformation by Seth and the horrors that followed.

Tasha's voice slices through the room's quietude. "So, are you a freak or what?" Her tone is casual, her focus unbroken on her drawing, not even glancing up at me.

I halt and fix Tasha with a stare. "I'm not a freak."

"Layla said you saw her transformation. That you read her mind."

"It's not like that." Or is it? Doubt creeps in. I'm unsure. I see things, yes, but what does that mean? I try to focus on the herbs, grinding them more intently and ignoring Tasha. It doesn't matter so much.

THE SOUND of the mortar and pestle fills the room, a welcome distraction from my spiralling thoughts and Tasha's unsettling question. Am I a freak? The thought troubles me, echoing a fear deep inside. Did my father see something in me that he despised?

"Why don't you like me?" I blurt out. It's not just her; it's been others too, in the death bringers' compound.

"I do like you," Tasha replies, her tone casual, almost indifferent.

"No, you don't. You've been against me since we first met."

Tasha's pencil halts, and she finally looks at me, her expression briefly revealing something enigmatic before she hides it behind a guarded facade. "And what makes you think that, Payton?"

I try to steady my trembling hands, still grinding herbs. "It's in the way you look at me, how you avoid me. It feels like jealousy." I regret the words as soon as they're out, but it's too late.

"Jealous? Don't flatter yourself," Tasha retorts sharply, leaning back and folding her arms defensively. "I'm not jealous of anything."

I lower my head, seeking refuge in silence. Picking another pot of herbs, I begin stripping the dried leaves, dropping them into the mortar. But Tasha's gaze burns into me, unsettling and intense.

Her eyes feel like daggers, cutting through the air. It's uncomfortable, like being scrutinised under a microscope. I try to block out her presence, focusing on the herbs, but it's challenging.

"You don't understand, do you?" Tasha's voice cuts through the quiet, sharp as a snapped twig. "It's not about jealousy. It's about survival."

Survival? The word looms large, casting a shadow over the room. I stop, the mortar and pestle now forgotten, as I process her words. What does she mean by survival?

Tasha leans forward, frustration and desperation mixing in her eyes. "Everything was fine before you came. We had our balance—us at the club, Killian and Naneve at their base. Then you show up and ..." Her voice wavers, betraying her emotions. "We were all fine."

Her words hit me hard, tightening a knot in my chest. My hands shake more noticeably. Tasha's accusation feels like a direct attack on the fragile connection I thought we were building.

"I didn't ask to be here," I murmur, my voice so low it's almost lost in the room. "I didn't choose any of this."

"But you chose to stay." She picks up her pad, but instead of resuming her drawing, she stands up abruptly, her glare piercing. "Tell Seth I'm in my room when he gets back. I'm sure he'll want to feed."

Her words hang in the air as she leaves, leaving me to grapple with the complex mix of emotions her departure stirs within me.

CHAPTER
THIRTY-SIX

Tasha only appears for our meal. Elena has prepared dinner, and Theo is still resting. The stew she's made fills the room with a warm, comforting aroma. Elena bakes the bread herself, fresh and warm. We spread butter on it, which melts into the bread, enriching its flavour.

Tasha enters, collects her food, and leaves without sitting with me. I pause, my spoon idly stirring the chunks of vegetables and tender meat in my bowl, the flavours barely registering.

"She doesn't mean to be so harsh," Elena offers, sitting across from me.

I meet her gaze. "Yes, she does, but it's okay," I respond, trying to sound unaffected. I'm used to it. Or at least I think I am. I can handle the hostility and the hurtful words. It's the constant tension and conflict that wears me down. "The stew is good," I say, steering the conversation away and glancing at the clock. Killian and Seth should be returning soon. Through the window, I notice the sky changing colours, heralding a new day.

I yearn for the sunrise, for the chance to sleep. Exhaustion envelops me, not just physically, but deep within. I'm tired of everything.

We eat mostly in silence, likely my fault. I don't have much to say, and Elena seems preoccupied, tallying the bags I filled. "What are you making?" I ask curiously if only to have conversation.

"Some healing bags, mainly for Theo. They'll help fight infection and aid his recovery," she explains as a timer goes off.

I finish my meal, soak up the last of the stew with my bread, and take my bowl to the sink. "Leave that. Take this to Theo. I'll clean up," Elena instructs, nodding towards the monitor. "Looks like they're back." My heart flutters at the sight of the gates opening on the screen. Seth is back.

Watching the monitor, my heart skips a beat as Seth dismounts some kind of vehicle. A quad bike, I think.

His presence, his confident stride, sends a wave of emotion through me.

Elena hands me the tray with Theo's healing bags, giving me an encouraging smile. "Go on."

I don't want to, but I nod, take the tray and head down the corridor, the wooden floor creaking under my steps, resonating in the quiet hallway. Reaching Theo's door, I take a deep breath and knock gently.

Theo's voice invites me in. I enter to find him on his side, his back bandaged and treated, a weary but grateful smile on his face.

"Elena sent dinner for you," I say, offering the tray.

"Put it on that table and then move it over to me."

I place the tray on the table as Theo instructs, then move both, noticing his pallid complexion and the slight wince of pain as he shifts. "How are you feeling?" I ask, concern evident in my tone.

He looks up with weary eyes. "I'm tired," he murmurs, his voice a faint whisper. "But I'll manage. Just need rest."

"You're a shifter?" I ask, curious.

"Half," he says, attempting to move but clearly in pain.

"Let me help." I assist him into a sitting position. The sores on his back seem to be festering rather than healing from what I can see. "What do you mean half? I thought …"

"My mother was a lycan, and my father was human."

I frown, puzzled. That isn't how I heard it all worked, but then what do I know? I'm so out of touch with everything. "I thought you were either a shifter or not," i say anyway, even if it sounds stupid.

"So they say, but it turns out there's a middle ground, and that's me." He pauses.

"Do you shift?"

"Never?"

He shakes his head. "No. I can sense the animal inside me, but I've never managed the transition. Would be cool, though, to transform and roam free." He shuffles to lean over the table and scoops some stew into his mouth. "This is good, not as great as mine, of course." He meets my gaze. "How about you? How are you coping?"

I wrap my arms around myself. "I'm okay."

"It's all pretty crazy, right?"

"Very crazy."

"Tasha mentioned you were a blood slave?" His gentle smile softens the question, but I'm sure I wince at the words. That question was always loaded with something else. "I'm just asking. We all have roles in this world the creatures have crafted."

"You don't have a liking for vampires?" I ask.

"Not particularly," Theo admits.

I frown again. I'm sure by now there is a perpetual crease in my forehead. "But you work for Seth."

He chuckles. "Ah, well, he's the exception, isn't he?"

I observe Theo for a moment as he eats. "Why?" I'm curious about his reasons.

He tears off a piece of bread, lathering it with butter. "Elena always skimps on this, says I'm getting too fat." He pats his belly. "Does this look too fat to you? Never mind, don't answer that. Anyway, Seth ..." Another pause, and this time he watches me. "Let me turn the question around. Does he act like any vampire you've ever known?"

I bite my lip, shaking my head. "Everything about him is different."

"Isn't it?."

"But why is that?"

"Aye, lass, that's not for me to say," he responds, then motions for me to sit. I do, finding comfort in Theo's easygoing nature. Elena is more guarded, Tasha is ... complicated, and then there's Layla. I've been trying to avoid her, afraid of setting her off again. It's on Theo's mind too, because he says, "Tell me about what you saw in the kitchen with Layla."

I shift uncomfortably. It feels unreal to me and even stranger to explain it. "You mean, when Seth turned her?"

"Yes. You saw the moment?"

I nod. "I don't know why, but I saw ..." I saw things I don't understand. But, despite that, I explain the vision to him, and he probes for every detail, picturing it in his mind.

When I finish, Theo falls silent for a long moment. "Have you had this happen before?"

"With the thirsty," I begin. "Yes. Two times and I ..." He

raises his eyebrows, encouraging me to continue, "And with Seth—"

But at that moment, the door opens, and I stop talking. It's Seth.

Seth enters the room with an effortless ease, his gaze immediately finding mine. A subtle smile graces his lips, causing my heart to flutter. His presence seems to fill the space, drawing my attention so completely that everything else momentarily fades into the background. He drops a bag beside Theo's bed. "Managed to get some of what you wanted from the hospital's desk, but it was locked up and darkness isn't on our side. We'll go back tomorrow for the rest. How are you holding up?"

I take this as my cue to leave. "I should head to bed," I say, feeling the weight of Seth's eyes on me as I stand up.

His gaze lingers on me as I move, a tangible force that seems to draw me towards him. My heart pounds, a rapid drumbeat in my chest, as I try to maintain my composure under his intense scrutiny. His very presence stirs something deep within me, awakening sensations I struggle to understand.

I nod to Theo, then glance back at Seth before exiting the room, his gaze still following me.

Stepping into the dim hallway, I'm engulfed by a flood of emotions. The memory of Seth's gaze, so full of intensity and unspoken desire, lingers on my skin, igniting a warmth that spreads through my body. The hallway's quietness contrasts starkly with the turmoil inside me.

Leaning against the cool wall, I press a hand to my chest, feeling my heartbeat race uncontrollably. My mind whirls with thoughts, each one laced with the electrifying memory of Seth's look—a look that seemed to penetrate right to my soul.

CHAPTER
THIRTY-SEVEN

Restlessness grips me as I return Theo's plate and bowl to the kitchen, now shrouded in darkness. The stove is off, pots cleaned and stored away, and whatever Elena was concocting has vanished.

Leaning against the sink, I gaze out the window, absorbing the rare luxury of witnessing the sunrise. Outside, Killian is busy in a shed or garage, storing away the quads he and Seth used. The scene, bathed in the soft morning light, is oddly calming.

I turn on the tap, placing the plate and bowl in the sink, embracing the quiet and the faint blue hue of dawn filtering through the window.

As I lose myself in the serenity of the moment, a breeze brushes against my skin, sending a shiver down my spine. Footsteps behind me break the tranquillity, my heart skipping a beat. I turn to find Seth standing there, a presence both imposing and comforting.

Our eyes meet, and time seems to pause. The air between us crackles with an unspoken intensity, drawing us inexorably closer. Seth's gaze holds a blend of longing and vulnerability that echoes my own tumultuous emotions.

Wordlessly, he steps towards me, his movements smooth and purposeful. A gentle smile touches his lips as he brushes a stray strand of hair from my face. His touch sends a current of anticipation through me, igniting every sense.

Captivated by his nearness, I barely notice as he reaches around me to pull down the blind, shielding us from the sunlight that could harm him. He steps back, creating a space between us that does nothing to dampen the rapid pounding of my heart.

I swallow hard, struggling to find my voice. "Did you find what you needed?"

"Aye," he replies simply, his gaze never leaving mine.

In the silence, the tension between us grows thicker, charged with unspoken desires. My pulse races in response to his nearness, my body aching for the connection that ignites whenever he is close.

The sensation is disconcerting. How could I feel this way about a vampire, about any of their kind? My experiences with them have only ever been marked by cruelty. So, this connection with Seth, it defies everything I know.

"Will we go to St Mary's tomorrow?" I ask, trying to shift the focus.

"It's too dangerous at night. Too many thirsty in the area. We'll need another plan," he responds, his gaze intense even in the dim light filtering from the corridor. "Tell me about what happened with Layla?"

As I meet his eyes, a whirlwind of words spins in my head, yet articulating them feels impossible. "I don't understand it myself," I admit. "It's like the girl on the stairs. I saw her final moments, her pain, what happened to her. And I saw you. You turned her. You fed her."

"That's how we turn people." He pauses to watch me and I feel so open, like a book he can read. I swallow, hard. He doesn't seem to notice the effect on me. "Have you always had these visions?"

I shake my head. "I had nothing." People with magic are rare. Witches, vampires, shifters exist, but those with telepathy, telekinesis … they're on a different level. "I don't understand where this comes from."

"What do you see when you touch me?"

My heart races, sure right then that he's going to come closer, going to close the gap. "It's different with you."

Seth steps towards me, his movements impossibly graceful, a predator stalking his prey. "How?" I catch a whiff of his scent, a heady mix of musk and woodsmoke that goes straight to my head. My heartbeat quickens in anticipation as our bodies brush against each other, electricity zinging through every nerve ending. His hand brushes my jawline, sending tingles down my spine. He's so close now that I can see the flecks of red in his eyes, like tiny stars caught in an endless abyss. With a sigh, he leans in and whispers against my ear, "Tell me what you see." A shiver runs down my spine at his warm breath on my neck.

I try to focus on what's different about seeing him—the way he holds himself, poised like a panther ready to pounce but also strangely vulnerable as if waiting for approval or judgement. His eyes reflect centuries of experiences, both joyful and haunting. He's seen so much more than any mortal should ever see; it's etched into every line on his face and every movement he makes. And yet there's something endearing about him too, something that makes me want to reach out and touch those lines, to smooth them away like wrinkles on an old map.

"I see your life before you were turned. I see your brother, you, Katherine."

At the mention of Katherine, Seth's face contorts with pain, his eyes fill with a mix of remorse and longing. "Katherine ..." His voice is raw, laden with emotion.

Instinctively, I reach out, placing a hand on his arm in a gesture of comfort. "I'm sorry," I whisper, my voice barely audible. "I didn't mean to stir up painful memories."

He searches my eyes for something elusive. "You do not understand."

The weight of my ignorance feels overwhelming, my heart pounding in response. "What don't I understand?"

He shakes his head, his eyes still locked on mine. "It is another story for another day." He huffs out a breath. "We should rest."

"What if you drink from me?" I ask suddenly, and the question hangs in the air, a suggestion filled with possibilities and unanswered questions. I can't take it back now.

Seth's reaction is immediate, a subtle recoil. "I won't drink from you."

"But you can. I ..."

"I didn't bring you here to be like the others before you. You're not here for me to feed from."

"It's not like that. You walked in the sunlight after drinking from me, right? My blood ... it did something?"

Seth's eyes widen, a mix of surprise and contemplation. His intense gaze pierces through me as he processes my words. His face, usually an emblem of composure, now displays a vivid struggle — desire clashing with hesitation.

"But I can't," he finally says, his voice echoing a deep,

unspoken ache. "I can't take from you. I refuse to use you in that way."

Despite the turmoil inside me, I step closer, my voice a mere whisper in the charged silence. "It's okay, though."

Our eyes lock, a world of emotions conveyed in a single glance. Seth's internal battle is evident, his sense of duty warring with the possibilities my words suggest. The air between us is thick with unsaid words and unexplored paths.

Seth's gaze penetrates deep into my soul, full of a longing and a question that I can't quite decipher. He reaches out slowly, his fingers lightly brushing my cheek with a tenderness that sends a shiver down my spine. "If I drink from you this time, it changes everything," he says with a gravitas that belies the gentle touch.

As he draws me closer, I feel the warmth of his breath against my skin, and his whispered words resonate within me, "I will never hurt you."

"I'm not afraid," I assure him, feeling a surprising calm amidst the rapid pounding of my heart. I go to him, offering myself.

Our lips meet in a kiss that is slow, yet filled with an intensity that seems to set my very soul alight. The world around us recedes into nothingness as we become lost in the moment. The kiss deepens, our connection growing with a hunger that is both new and as old as time itself.

Seth's hands explore gently, his touch conveying a depth of emotion that words could never capture. Each caress along my skin feels like a discovery, an expression of love and reverence. As his fingers trace the curve of my waist, a shiver of desire courses through me.

I respond instinctively, my fingers weaving through his dark hair, pulling him closer, deepening our connection.

The sensation of his taste is overwhelming, a heady mix that intoxicates my senses. The closeness between us ignites a fire that seems to consume every fibre of my being.

His lips trail a path down to my neck, scattering soft kisses. Instinctively, I tilt my head back, offering him greater access to my skin, which yearns for his touch. He alternates between gentle nips and soothing licks, sending waves of pleasure through me.

My body naturally arches towards him, craving his touch. Seth's hands glide over my body, his touch on my skin igniting a deep, primal hunger within me. The world around us fades, leaving only our intertwined forms in a passionate dance.

As Seth's lips find their way across my chest, every touch sends shivers of delight coursing through me. I arch into his embrace, surrendering to the intoxicating sensations.

Seth's hands wander lower, exploring with reverence. He pulls me closer, our bodies melding into one. The intensity of our connection builds with every urgent movement.

Suddenly, I feel the slight prick of his fangs. It's a sensation of both pleasure and pain, thrilling yet gentle. My breath hitches in anticipation.

Seth's fangs sink in gently. It's an ecstasy like none other, a mix of pain and profound pleasure. Our connection deepens, souls intertwining in this intimate act. It's exhilarating and terrifying, a precarious balance between pleasure and danger.

As Seth drinks, time and the world dissolve into the background. We are lost in this primal, forbidden ritual, a symbiotic dance of predator and prey. I surrender to him, willingly caught in the pull of his embrace.

Gradually, my strength wanes under the spell of his

draw, but there's no fear, only surrender to the overwhelming ecstasy.

Then he stops, pulling back slightly. He lifts his face to mine, forehead to forehead, his eyes piercing into mine. "Thank you," he whispers, his voice a soft murmur filled with gratitude and a depth of emotion that resonates within my very core.

CHAPTER
THIRTY-EIGHT

We stand together in the kitchen, the morning sun attempting to peek through the edges of the blind, yet unable to penetrate fully.

Seth, next to me, appears different, and I can feel the change. His presence inside me has grown stronger, distinctly altered since he first drank my blood. He stands with his shirt open, his chest bare. Watching him breathe in, I've grown accustomed to the oddity of it. He nods to the blind. "Open it slowly."

I reach out, pressing the button that controls the shutters. They wind up with a mechanical whir, gradually lifting the blind. Instinctively, Seth steps back, as if expecting the sunlight to blaze through and sear him as it once did.

His burns have healed, his former majestic appearance restored. But even as the blind continues to rise, he retreats further into the shadows as if afraid, only stopping when he's backed to the table.

He takes in another breath. "I don't feel it," he

murmurs, a note of wonder in his voice. In moments like these, a different side of Seth emerges.

Around others, he exudes power and resolve, but here, with me, there's a vulnerability, a touch of humanity I've never seen in his kind before. It's a trait more common in young vampires, those recently turned, but he's allowing me to see this part of him, showing me what he would view as a weakness. .

I remain silent, simply observing him. He extends a hand, daring to place it in the ray of sunlight filtering through, his fingers intersecting the motes of dust dancing in the beam.

When I touched Layla, only her turning unfolded before me, but with Seth, it's different. Now, I see the man hidden within him. Despite centuries passing, he has clung to his humanity—loving, kind, and full of dignity. He embodies honour and morals, everything his brother is not.

Seth cautiously extends his arm into the sunlight, and it gently caresses his skin. I realise I've been holding my breath, releasing it only when he exhales his relief. "Nothing," he says, a hint of disbelief in his voice. "I feel nothing." He then steps fully into the light, allowing it to cascade across his bare chest. Tilting his head back, he opens his mouth, revealing his fangs, yet there's a smile there—I'm certain of it. His face and skin are bathed in light, and he inhales deeply, as if savouring a lungful of fresh air for the first time.

As he lowers his head, bringing his arms in to examine his hands, he looks at them as though seeing them anew. "It's the most amazing thing," he says, his eyes locking with mine. "I feel like I'm alive."

He steps out of the shadow completely, allowing the

sunlight to envelop him. "I've spent centuries in darkness," he whispers, almost to himself.

Killian enters through the back door, leading directly into the utility room and then the kitchen. His face is already etched with shock before he fully steps in.

"What are you doing ..." He goes to rush towards Seth, as if to shield him from the sunlight, but then halts abruptly, the realisation dawning on him. "You're not burning." His eyes then shift to me, narrowing as they land on the marks on my neck from Seth's bite. I instinctively cover them with my hand.

He turns to face Killian, and there is a smile. Ne so strong but so human like, it catches me off guard, making my heart race. "It doesn't burn me."

Killian eyes over Seth, then his attention is on me. "He fed from you?"

I nod. "We wanted to try it, to see what would happen."

"We can proceed to St. Mary's now," Seth says, as if this had always been the plan, and Killian was merely lagging behind in understanding.

Any questions Killian has, or comments he wants to make, falter and die on his lips as he looks between me and Seth, then back again.

Seth straightens his shoulders, beginning to button up his shirt with a newfound sense of purpose. "Get Naneve," he commands Killian. "Tell her we're heading out while the sun is still up." He turns to me with a determined look. "This is a gift from you. I will never ask for more or expect it."

CHAPTER
THIRTY-NINE

We're preparing to use quad bikes, a mode of transport I haven't encountered since childhood, and only then on television. Seth's property harbours a large building filled with various vehicles, including cars, bikes, and notably, Killian's large bike that he's currently working on.

Standing in the garden, I shield my eyes from the glaring sun, trying to gauge the expanse of land stretching back to the distant wall. The estate is vast, its boundaries lost in the distance.

Killian and Naneve are busy pulling out the quads, lining them up in an orderly fashion. Naneve, with her typical scowl, pushes one towards me before retreating back inside.

"There's an extra quad," I observe. "Who's it for?" There are five in total, not four, for me, Naneve, Killian, and Seth.

"Elena is joining us," Seth explains. "She used to be a lab technician. With her ideas for testing, she's the best for the job."

"A witch who was a lab technician?" I blurt out,

surprised by my own forwardness. My comment halts the others in their tracks.

Killian stops and narrows his eyes. "What makes you think she's a witch?"

I take a step back, more out of instinct than fear. "All the herbs and remedies she uses," I reply, though I realise it's not just that. After all, she's not the only one to brew remedies in this world, not when medication is so scarce. Desperate people try anything.

But Killian considers my response for a moment, then nods, accepting it. It doesn't really matter what I think or why.

"Do you really think we'll find answers?" Naneve asks, her glare full of the usual contempt.

"Aye, I do," Seth responds confidently.

Naneve's stare is intense, as if she wants to say more, but I don't prompt her. Even though I've changed since Seth chose me at the auction, parts of me still shy away from confrontation.

"Where's Elena?" Naneve finally asks instead.

"Making sure Theo has everything he needs before we leave," Killian answers.

"Will he be okay on his own?"

"Aye," Seth replies, his voice carrying a hint of amusement. "Theo would be fine on his own without the help, but he humours Elena's fussing."

I stand back, observing Seth, Naneve, and Killian as they efficiently prepare for the journey. They've tended to the quads out, fueled them, and are now checking over weapons on a small table set between them. Seth's movements catch my attention; he seems different somehow, as if he's pulsing with a newfound vitality. Always a figure of power and control, now there's an added element, a sense of being truly alive that emanates from him. It's a stark contrast to Layla's vampire aura, which carries a distinct signature of undeath, an eerie sense of being perpetually reborn.

I asked one of the girls at Crevan's place if she felt the same energy from vampires. Her baffled look made me realise not everyone senses it, so I never brought it up again.

"Will he be alright with Layla?" I ask, thinking of Theo left alone in the house. It is one thing to be able to care for himself, but having a half-starved vampire who is desperate for blood, is another.

"The sunlight has calmed her. She won't wake until darkness falls," Seth assures me, referring to Layla's vampire nature.

My gaze drifts back towards the building, feeling eyes on me. It's probably Tasha, watching from somewhere within.

The quad bikes are neatly arranged and ready for our departure. Compact in design, they're clearly meant for solo riders. From this, it's evident that Seth has meticulously prepared for this day, or a day like it, having everything in its place, from the quad bikes to the bunker room at Skin Trade. He knew war was coming.

Even the house. Elena and Theo were the only residents before our arrival, a strategic decision by Seth, no doubt. Fewer confidants mean less risk of betrayal. This secluded estate must also serve as Seth's refuge from the demanding life of a vampire king.

We mount the quads, with Seth and Killian leading. They're deep in discussion, strategizing our route. Despite Seth's newfound ability to walk in sunlight, we aren't keen on testing his limits. We'll travel through shadows and hidden paths, using trees for cover, choosing routes that offer safety.

The drawback of these shadowy paths is the potential presence of the thirsty, but we expect to encounter only a few, not hordes.

Next to me, Naneve effortlessly climbs onto her quad, her long legs stretching out, her heavy boots planted firmly on the ground. I can't help but feel a bit out of place among them. Dressed in simple leggings and trainers, with a thick coat against the cold, I seem distinctly civilian next to their readiness for battle. Killian, in his black combat trousers tucked into sturdy boots, and Naneve, both embody the soldier's readiness for combat.

Elena emerges from the kitchen's back door, her attire striking a balance between combat readiness and casual practicality. She sports her version of combat trousers and sturdy walking shoes, resembling a mother ready to chaperone a children's outdoor activity.

"How's Theo this morning?" Seth inquires, concern evident in his voice.

"He's struggling without proper medication. The herbs are helping, but slowly. He's in pain," Elena replies.

Seth nods, his response firm. "I'm sure We'll find what's needed at St Mary's so you can properly treat him."

A kind of silent understanding passes between them as Elena mounts her bike, pulling it from the shed's shadow and flinging off its cover. Her bike, dented and battle-worn, suggests a long history of similar outings. She aligns it with ours, inserting keys into the ignition.

My knowledge of mechanics is limited. My childhood was filled with dolls and toys, the intricacies of vehicles never caught my interest. My father handled that aspect of our lives, relegating cars to mere tools for transportation. The most I did was help him fill the fuel tank in my younger years.

Naneve, breaking into my thoughts, tosses a set of keys to me. I clumsily try to catch them, but they clatter to the ground. Leaning over to retrieve them, I almost slide off the quad, eliciting an eye roll and an audible sigh from her, her displeasure at my lack of coordination apparent.

Taking the keys Naneve tossed to me, I'm uncertain which one to use but choose the largest, imitating the others as I insert it into the ignition. Grasping the handle grip, I feel the bike shift slightly under my hand. I mimic Naneve's actions, pressing the pedal and twisting the handle. The bike sputters to life, jerks forward, then stalls, the engine cutting out.

Naneve's impatience is evident. "You can't even do this? What did you do in your pampered life?"

"I wasn't allowed outside," I respond, my voice steady. It's not an excuse, but a fact. My life under Craven, while fraught with horrors, was also incredibly sheltered. We were kept hidden, our movements restricted and controlled, far from the normality of riding bikes or having any freedom.

"You've never ridden a bike?" Seth asks, a hint of amusement in his tone, devoid of Naneve's bitterness. It seems he momentarily forgot the constraints of my previous life. He wheels his bike back to mine, positioning it so closely our legs touch. "This is the throttle," he explains, guiding my hand to the part of the handle I'd twisted. "You need to twist it to keep the bike going. The foot pedal powers the bike too. It's straightforward." He indicates the brake levers. "Use the left one more than the right, or you'll end up over the handlebars. We'll go slow."

He addresses the others, especially Naneve, outlining our formation. "Naneve will lead, Killian behind, then Elena, and I'll ride beside you."

Seth's patient explanation eases some of my apprehension. There's a comfort in his proximity, a reassurance in his presence.

Following his directions, I start the bike successfully, avoiding the earlier jolt. We set off, heading along the winding path that led to Seth's house. Instead of retracing our previous route, we venture in a new direction, skirting the property's expansive wall. Its sheer length amazes me, stretching miles around the estate.

Emerging onto a narrow dirt track, our journey to the hospital is considerably shorter than the trip from Skin Trade. We navigate through shadows and trees, veering off the path occasionally. The derelict park we cross, with its rusted gates and overgrown bandstand, speaks of a forgotten era. Nature has reclaimed the once-vibrant space, entwining itself around the structures. The remnants of a bygone age – an ice cream stand, a boat rental booth – are now hollow shells, their former glory ravaged by time and neglect.

The presence of ducks on a large, desolate lake surprises me. Decaying paddle boats hint at happier times when families might have enjoyed leisurely afternoons here. We ride around the lake, under the cover of trees, over broken paths, and across stone bridges spanning the water.

The road leading to the hospital is just as damaged as the rest of the landscape, with the sun's heat warping the tarmac. Non-functioning traffic lights are entangled in overgrowth. The hospital itself, with its faded sign, stands as a testament to the devastation that has swept through the area.

Seth signals for us to halt. We align in formation, with me positioned in the middle. "Killian and I didn't get far inside last night," Seth explains. "There may be thirsty lurking, so stay vigilant."

Naneve unsheathes her blade, ready for confrontation. Killian and even Elena reveal their weapons – hers noticeably smaller than Killian's massive blade.

A sudden realisation hits me. "I forgot my weapons," I admit, panic rising. I had left the belt Seth gave me, with its attached knives, back at the house.

"Of course, you did," Naneve says.

Naneve's remark elicits a sharp look from Seth, but he remains silent, focusing on the task at hand. "You won't need them," he reassures me, indicating the hospital building. He outlines our plan: entering through the car park and heading straight to the pathology department to gather necessary tools and supplies.

Elena's attention is on the nearby pharmacy and lab, where she might find useful items.

In formation, we cross the road, led by Killian who knows the layout. We park the quads in a smaller car park, noticing signs reserved for doctors, a reminder of those who might have fallen victim to the thirsty or the virus.

Seth leads the way, guiding us with a familiarity that seems almost innate. The hospital, despite its abandoned state, retains that distinct antiseptic scent, now tinged with the smell of decay.

We cautiously navigate through what was once the reception area, now a scene of disarray with overturned chairs and shattered seating. Seth confidently moves through the corridors as if he's walked them countless times before.

As we proceed, our eyes stay alert for any lurking thirsty. We find a room, what was once some kind of examination room. It's relatively untouched. Seth and Elena rummage through drawers and cabinets in search of useful items, while Killian and Naneve stand guard. I would help to look, but I think I'll only get in their way, so I stay back, not touching, peering at fading posters on the wall. This had to be some kind of general office from what I can see.

"Found one," Elena says, holding up a sealed package with a needle in it. But the way they look at each other, sets me on edge. There's something they're not telling me. "What's going on?"

It's Naneve who answers, though not for me. She addresses Seth and Elena. "You're going to test her blood on a thirsty?" Her voice reflects a mix of surprise and concern. "That's what you were talking about before?" I hadn't heard that conversation, but she must have. I'm sure there are many discussions and decisions I have missed.

Still, it takes me by surprise. "My blood?"

"It's an idea we had," Seth says. "Give them your blood in a controlled manner. See what happens."

I look around at the group. I could be upset about this plan, but surprisingly, I'm not. In all of this, that makes sense. They crave it, hunt me for it. It allows Seth to walk in the sun, so what would it do for one of them? It takes me a moment, but I nod and frown. "So, we need to find one?"

Seth shakes his head. "Killian and I captured one last night."

My eyes widen. "You caught a thirsty?"

"It's locked in a secured room and restrained."

Elena has the needle on the counter and she's managed

to find a bunch of small vials—vials the hospitals would send specimens in. I put my hand to my arm. iIt's been a long time since anyone took blood for me in a normal manner.

"You don't have to do this if you don't want," Seth says.

"But it'll help us to understand," adds Elena.

"No. I want to. I want to know what will happen." I take off my jacket and then pull up my sleave, offering Elena my arm.

She takes three full vials of my blood. "This should be enough."

"I want you to stay here," Seth says to me. His concern is evident. "I don't want you in any danger, especially not near a thirsty. Naneve can stay with you."

I feel a surge of determination. "I want to come. I want to see. You said it's restrained."

"It is," he confirms.

"Then I want to see." My voice is firm. I'm a part of this now, and I need to understand fully what's happening, even if it means facing a thirsty. I think it s time I stopped hiding in the shadows and take my true place in this world, but I am not yet sure were that is.

CHAPTER
FORTY

The thirsty is confined in a room, its door secured with an axe handle jammed into the handle. From the small window, the others can glimpse inside, but they keep me shielded from view, nestled securely between them.

"It's still secured," Killian confirms to Seth, blade at the ready. Naneve, equally prepared, unsheathes her own sword.

Seth carefully removes the axe handle, gripping it as a potential weapon. As he opens the door, the room's vile stench assaults us. Covering my mouth with my sleeve, I can barely stifle a whisper of disgust at the overwhelming odours of death, urine, and other indescribable scents.

Despite the stench, I follow them into the dark room. Killian holds out a hand, signalling me to wait as the thirsty hisses and gasps inside.

Naneve moves to the window, allowing just enough light to spill in, forcing the thirsty to recoil from the sunlight. Its shrieks pierce the air, adding to the already unbearable atmosphere. I cover my ears, trying to block out the noise.

Killian stays close, his blade ready, while Naneve and Seth ensure the thirsty is still securely tied to a chair. The creature, a woman with long, matted blond hair and glazed eyes, is visibly wasting away, a common trait among her kind. Tattoos cover one arm, hinting at a life she once led.

"Am I to touch her?" I ask, aware of the numerous tests and understandings we need to unravel.

"You will," Seth replies. "But first, we need to see what happens when we give her this." He motions Elena.

Between them, Naneve and Seth hold the thirsty's arm, extending it as Elena prepares to administer my blood. The thirsty hisses and struggles, her glazed eyes fixed on me with a deep hunger.

I shift slightly, drawing her attention, guiding her gaze away from Seth and Elena's actions. I don't want her to lash out at them.

Killian's voice breaks through her hisses, "She's following you, just like the others."

"Yes," I reply, anticipation lacing my words, "I'm hoping she will."

Elena swiftly inserts the needle into the vampire's arm, her movements precise and calculated. As she depresses the plunger, the creature struggles, its body tensed against the unknown intrusion. But then, unexpectedly, the resistance fades. The fierce snarl that had been etched on its face begins to distort, gradually dissolving into an expression of confusion.

Seth moves to put Elena behind him, unsure of what the thirsty is going to do. We all watch her intently, ready for something, because she's stilled. She frowns, her gaze darting around in bewilderment, landing on us but devoid of the usual savage hunger. Her mouth, normally agape in a feral snarl, now closes quietly.

We stand together, holding our breath, witnessing a flicker of humanity wash over her.

"Should we open the other blinds?" Naneve asks tentatively. The creature, bound to a chair beneath the window, seems less of a monster now and more of the woman she must have been before the sickness claimed her. .

"Just a little," Seth instructs, his voice a blend of caution and curiosity. "We're not trying to kill her. We're trying to understand."

As Naneve cautiously adjusts the blind, sunlight slips into the room, casting a revealing glow. The creature doesn't flinch or recoil but watches the light touch her skin with a mixture of fear and wonder.

Elena covers her mouth in disbelief, her eyes wide. Her bewilderment mirroring everyone's. "It's not burning her."

Seth steps closer, an air of fascination surrounding him. The creature looks up, her eyes locking with his. There's a moment of silent communication, a shared understanding.

"What does this mean now?" Naneve asks, the room now bathed in sunlight. "She should be dead."

Seth's doesn't take his eyes off the woman, "What it means is that we need to protect Payton from my brother. With her blood ..."

"He'd be stronger," I finish for him.

I edge closer, drawn in by the woman's presence. Who was she before this cursed existence? These thoughts always stir a sense of sorrow within me.

Seth doesn't stop me but stands tall, watching over both of us.

"Can I touch her?" I ask, the urge surging within me. There's a pull, a need to connect, to feel her skin and understand her transformation.

Killian steps beside me, his blade at the ready for any sudden strike. Seth nods at us, a silent signal of readiness.

The vampire, once thrashing in her bonds, now sits eerily still. I'm puzzled by her sudden calm. Crouching, I bring myself to her level, our eyes meeting. Her gaze is haunting - empty yet seemingly all-seeing. The filmy glaze over her eyes suggests blindness, but she appears acutely aware of my presence.

Gently, I extend my hand towards her, enveloping her cold, fragile hand in mine. It's an experience reminiscent of my encounter with Layla. I catch my breath, my eyes fluttering shut, as her vivid memory transports me to another room, another moment. I steady my breathing, feeling the pressure in my chest, fighting against the pull of the memory.

"Hold my hand," I murmur. Seth moves to respond, but I shake my head, gesturing to Killian instead. His strong grip around my hand anchors me, his living essence steadying the turmoil within me.

"What do you see?" he asks.

Closing my eyes again, I let the vision envelop me. "She's in a hotel room," I describe, my voice a whisper. "There's a fire safety sign on the wall, the usual impersonal hotel decor. But she's not just lying there - she's tied to the bed, her body a canvas of horror." My voice breaks as the scene unfolds, each detail sharper, more grotesque.

"She isn't alone. There are men, five vampires, and they're restraining a young one, about her age. He's struggling, resisting them. They're forcing him towards her. One of them lifts her skirt, carelessly slices her skin, letting the blood trickle down. He drinks from the wound. They all do, one after another, cutting, drinking, biting. Her screams fill the room, but there's no salvation. They drain her life, her essence, and then ..." My voice trails off, the horror too much to bear.

I release my grip, the vision fading, leaving behind a chilling echo of despair. I stagger backwards, my balance faltering, but Seth is there in an instant. His hands grasp mine, a steady anchor in the storm of emotions. The connection with Killian is severed; I've recoil from both him and the vampire.

"They forced her transformation," I gasp, the words heavy with realisation, "then exploited her."

Elena's voice cuts through the tension. "Is that all you see? Just the moment of her turning?"

My eyes find Seth. With him, the visions are different, deeper. With others, it's merely glimpses. "I don't know," I admit, the uncertainty gnawing at me. "Maybe it's only different with Seth. I've never actually seen the exact moment he was turned, only pieces of his life leading up to it."

"Would you try again?" Elena urges gently.

Nodding, I approach the vampire, this time alone, without Killian's or her touch. I'm ready to delve deeper, to look through this small window into her last memory.

The moment my skin makes contact, I'm yanked back into her world. It's like with Layla, a golden thread of light, stretching from her heart to mine. I glance down at my own form, seeing the light connecting to my heart, pulsating in sync with my own heartbeat.

I trace the ethereal thread with my gaze, then my

hands. It feels like the softest feathers, light and delicate. As I touch it fully, then pull. A burst of light radiates from my hands, coursing through my body. Then, a resounding pop echoes through my mind, as if it had occurred outside my own head.

I jolt back, losing my footing, and this time, Seth is the only thing keeping me from falling. His arms envelop me, his presence a reassuring comfort.

The vampire in the chair slumps, her arms dangling limply, head lolling back. A wave of despair washes over me as I bring my hand to my mouth, the realisation hitting me like a physical blow.

"Oh no," I whisper, my voice choking with horror. "I killed her."

Chapter
Forty-One

Donovan looms over the book, its presence now a constant torment in his life. Ever since he learnt of its existence, the book with its thick, red cover – seemingly crafted from some peculiar skin – has fascinated and frustrated him in equal measure. The cover feels unnaturally warm to his touch as he flips it open, only to be met with blank pages. Yet, he senses the magic within it, a life force pulsating just out of reach.

Marcus lounges on the sofa, his latest victim sprawled across his lap. The casual way he laps at the blood oozing from her throat creates a macabre backdrop to Donovan's concentration. The rhythmic sucking sound punctuates the silence, grating on Donovan's nerves.

Exasperated, Donovan snaps, "For God's sake, can't you feed quietly?"

Marcus pauses, lifting his head, his chin and lips glistening with the woman's blood. "You insist we stay awake, then I must feed."

"We all stay awake until this puzzle is solved," Donovan retorts, his patience wearing thin.

"And you're the one bleeding all over the place," Marcus counters with a sneer.

Donovan touches his nose, the back of his hand coming away with blood. He hastily wipes it away with a small cloth. Amelia has fed, Marcus is feeding, but Donovan resists. The blood sates their thirst temporarily, but like him, they too will succumb to the sun's deadly rays if they don't feed properly. Yet, Donovan's focus remains unwavering - he needs to unlock this book and its secrets for himself and for Payton.

Marcus, pushing his dazed victim aside, inquires, "What do you think will happen when you finally crack open that book?"

Donovan leans heavily on the table, lost in thought. "If the effects of the small taste of blood I had from her are anything to go by, then opening this book could give us control over everything."

In his mind, Donovan amends, 'I control everything', but he keeps this thought to himself. Marcus and Amelia, though powerful and more capable than most of their kind, are mere pawns in his grand plan. Marcus, especially, is driven by base desires, whereas Amelia at least possesses some intelligence.

Marcus's voice breaks his reverie, "What about her father?"

Donovan frowns, irritation creasing his brow. "What about her father?"

"He's her blood, right? Her biological father, as they call it. That means he shares at least fifty percent of her blood. You need blood to open that book, right?" Marcus questions, piecing together the puzzle.

Donovan considers this. He's deduced that the well on

the inside cover is the key – a magical lock, typical of a grimoire, sealed by a witch to be opened only by the witch herself or a descendant. A grin curls his lips as he recalls the night he slaughtered Katherine's mother, her blood sweet and rich. Yet, Payton's blood was even more exquisite, the crème de la crème.

"But he is her father, not her mother. Witches are female," Donovan points out, dismissing the idea.

Marcus rises, his latest victim sliding lifelessly to the floor. Her eyes are glazed over, blood seeping from the unsealed wound. She'll be dead within minutes.

"You're speaking in riddles again, Marcus," Amelia adds, moving to attend to the dying girl. She feels the urge herself, the sun's deadly rays outside calling to her, demanding a sip of blood to stave off death.

"No," Marcus persists. "Payton's father shares her blood. Use his to open the book, or to find her, to communicate with her." Because that is what vampires do. They need to have tasted the blood to be able to communicate. Powerful vampires can do it without, but it's draining, but for a better connection ... blood is always the answer.

Donovan had tried reaching out to Payton, but she was a void now, unreachable. "I need witch's blood."

"And he might have it. Have you even tried?" Marcus counters.

Donovan narrows his eyes, the frustration evident. "It won't work."

"But you don't know that. He could carry the dormant witch's power, passed on to his daughter. Her mother wasn't magical; she'd be alive if she were. The very power of the witches would have shielded her from Alitora," Marcus argues.

Realisation dawns on Donovan. "Which is why he survived, why he's still alive."

This new perspective sets Donovan's mind racing. A slow, calculating smile creeps across his face. "Get me Summers. We have much to discuss."

CHAPTER
FORTY-TWO

Restlessness grips me, its claws digging deep as I lie in my bed, the world outside bathed in sunlight. Time stretches endlessly, each tick of the clock echoing my inner turmoil. I'm back at the house, in the familiarity of my own room, yet it feels alien, the ceiling above a blank canvas for my troubled thoughts.

I replay the day's events, the weight of my actions crushing me. I didn't take her actual life, but I ended the one she had. My hands, once ordinary extensions of myself, now feel alien, tainted.

Restlessly, I toss and turn, the sheets twisting around me. The guilt is a relentless spectre, haunting every corner of my mind. The room feels like a prison, its silence suffocating.

Needing an escape, I rise shakily, the floorboards protesting under my tentative steps. The cool air of the hallway brushes against my skin, a fleeting respite from the oppressive guilt.

Approaching Seth's door, uncertainty gnaws at me. Fear

of his judgement battles with the need to see him, to seek solace in his presence. My hand trembles as I push open the door, revealing the darkness beyond.

Seth's room is a haven of soft light and calm. He sits there, a solitary figure immersed in a book, his hair falling in a shadow over his eyes. My heart flutters at the sight, a mix of apprehension and longing.

I move towards him, each creak of the floor announcing my approach. Seth looks up, his eyes reflecting surprise and something deeper.

"Payton," he greets me, his voice a soothing melody that eases my inner chaos.

"Seth," I reply, my voice a mere whisper in the stillness. I drink in his appearance, finding solace in the familiarity of his features and the empathy in his eyes.

He gestures to the space beside him, a wordless invitation. I'm drawn to him, each step feeling like a leap across an emotional chasm. As I sit, the mattress dips gently, enveloping us in a shared space of comfort and understanding.

He sets aside his book, turning his full attention to me. The room thrums with a strumming energy, every inch alive with the intensity of our connection.

"I've been waiting for you," Seth admits, his voice a soft whisper laced with longing.

His words envelop my heart, a gentle balm that begins to thaw the remorse that has held it captive. His understanding and patience feel like a haven in the storm of my guilt.

"I know she was just a thirsty, that she was already lost, but I ..." My voice falters as I present my hands, symbols of my deed. I can't bear to look at them, to truly acknowledge what they've done. "I ended her life. I ..."

"You ended her suffering," Seth says, his tone firm yet compassionate.

I nod slowly, allowing his perspective to seep into my consciousness, to challenge my self-condemnation.

Seth's hands envelop mine, his touch a conduit of warmth and reassurance. His eyes, deep and searching, seem to dive into the very essence of my being. "You didn't take her life," he insists gently. "She was already beyond reach, ensnared in a shell that was no longer hers. You liberated her from that agony, from the fetters that kept her tethered to a torturous existence."

A solitary tear escapes, trailing down my cheek, a silent testament to the mingled sorrow and solace I feel. "Is that what it feels like for you?" I ask, my voice thick with emotion. "Are you bound by chains to this world?"

Seth's eyes meet mine, and in them, I see a reflection of his own inner struggle, the silent battles he wages. "We all bear our own burdens in this world," he says, a note of resigned acceptance in his voice.

"You have lived a long time without Katherine," I murmur, recalling the age-worn headstone and its silent testimony. "You loved her deeply." The intensity of that love had resonated in my vision. "And she loved you."

Seth's gaze on me is thoughtful, tinged with a sorrow long-held. "She was not meant to be mine."

"But the heart wants what the heart wants," I say softly, understanding the truth of these words.

A bittersweet smile graces Seth's lips, his eyes reflecting a world of unfulfilled desires and silent yearnings. "Yes," he acknowledges, the word heavy with unspoken emotions.

I reach out, my fingertips gently tracing the line of his cheek. "And what does your heart want, Seth?"

For a moment, Seth's eyes close, his face leaning into

my caress as if drawing comfort from the simple touch. When he looks at me again, his eyes are pools of raw vulnerability, revealing the depths of his soul.

"I want you," he confesses, his voice a tremulous blend of longing and uncertainty.

Seth's fingers entwine with mine, anchoring me in this surreal moment. His thumb caresses the back of my hand, sending ripples of anticipation coursing through me.

The room is enveloped in a charged silence, thick with the tension of unspoken promises and shared desires. Every fibre of my being vibrates with anticipation and my heart beats a wild rhythm, urging me towards a future unknown yet irresistibly compelling.

"I'm here."

Without breaking eye contact, Seth leans in slowly, his lips just inches away from mine. His breath dances against my skin, warm and fragrant. It's a heady mixture of mint and sandalwood, intoxicating my senses and clouding my thoughts.

Heat radiates from his body, drawing me closer like a magnet and I can't stop myself, but this is not like with any of the men at Crevan's. This is something else. The weight of Seth's statement swirls around us like a tempestuous storm and with each passing second, the space between us diminishes, until finally our lips meet in a gentle and tentative kiss. Our mouths move together in perfect harmony, exploring and tasting one another with an urgency born out of years of longing.

My heart strums as the kiss deepens, our lips moulding against each other with increasing intensity. There is only the sweetness of his mouth against mine, the feel of his warm breath mingling with mine.

Seth's fangs graze against my lower lip, a subtle reminder of his true nature. A jolt of fear courses through me, but I find myself leaning into his touch. His kiss becomes more fervent, his lips trailing down my throat and collarbone, leaving a trail of wet heat in their wake.

"Seth ..." Waves of pleasure cascade through my body as his name escapes my lips. His teeth gently graze my skin, a light touch that amplifies the sensations rippling through me, sending shivers down my spine, until his hands roam over my curves, tracing each contour with a reverence that leaves me breathless.

His touch is both possessive and tender and as Seth's lips find their way back to mine, I taste the metallic tang of blood on his tongue. But there is no time to question it. The kiss intensifies, fueled by an undeniable hunger. His body presses against mine, the closeness speaking volumes of his longing and need.

His caresses grows bolder, his hands gliding up my sides and slipping beneath the fabric of my t-shirt. Every touch is a word in the unspoken language of our connection, each movement deepening the bond that pulls us inexorably together. He pulls away only to push my t-shirt up and pull it over my head.

The cool air in the room sends goosebumps across my skin, but then his fingers are tracing the contours of my breasts, teasingly circling the hardened peaks beneath my bra. "You are so beautiful," he murmurs. A soft moan escapes my lips, swallowed by the intensity of our kisses. Seth's touch is like fire on my skin, electrifying every nerve ending, setting me ablaze with desire.

He eases me back onto the bed, his lips never leaving mine. The weight of his body pressing against me, sends a surge of anticipation through my centre. A shiver runs down my spine as Seth's strong hands glide over my torso, inching closer to the clasp that holds my bra in place. I arch my back, silently urging him forward.

With expert precision, he unhooks the clasp and slowly reveals my breasts to his hungry gaze. His eyes darken with desire as he leans down to capture one peak in his mouth. The sensation of his warm, wet tongue swirling around my nipple sends pleasure straight to the core of my being.

As Seth's lips and tongue lavish attention on one breast, his hand kneads and caresses the other. But amidst the intoxication of desire, I catch a glimpse of vulnerability in his eyes. It's as if he's unravelling the layers of his own existence, allowing me to see beyond the seductive facade he wears. And in that moment, I understand that this connection is more than just physical gratification. It's a dance of souls, seeking solace and something I don't yet understand within each other.

I thread my fingers through his hair and guide him upwards, pulling him away from my breasts. "Should we be doing this?"

Between breathless kisses, words escape Seth's lips. "You can tell me to stop. You have a choice."

I look into his eyes. " I don't want you to stop."

Seth's eyes darken further with a mix of desire and relief. Then his hands are moving again, gliding to the waistband of my pants. His touch is both gentle and deliberate as he slowly begins to unbutton them, his fingers dancing over each button like a maestro playing an intricate melody.

With a soft gasp, I feel the fabric of my pants loosen around my hips, the cool air kissing the exposed skin beneath. Seth's hands slide down further, gliding over the curve of my hips. I suck in a breath, silently urging him to continue this journey of discovery.

His lips leave mine with a breathless sigh, planting kisses along the column of my neck. A shiver dances down my spine as his teeth graze against the sensitive skin, sending shockwaves of pleasure through my body. Every touch, every kiss, every nip of his fangs pulls me deeper into the abyss of passion.

With a sure hand, Seth slides his fingers beneath the waistband of my panties, teasingly tracing along the edge. The anticipation builds within me, the tension coiling tighter and tighter.

I bite my lip, fighting back a moan as his fingertips graze my most intimate area. The delicious friction makes me yearn for him even more—a hunger that can only be sated by his touch.

Seth's eyes meet mine as his fingers move with deliberate intent, slowly sliding my panties down my legs, revealing all of me to him. I am bare and vulnerable, exposed in body and soul. And yet, in this raw state, I feel an indescribable power.

He slides down my body and as his lips graze against the sensitive flesh of my inner thigh, it's as if every nerve ending in my body sings in harmony, attuned to the melody of his touch. I surrender myself completely to the symphony that unfolds between us, the rhapsody of moans and sighs that punctuates our movements.

His breath is warm against my skin as he inches closer to my core, his lips hovering tantalisingly close but never fully touching. It's a delicious torture, a game of desire and anticipation that leaves me teetering on the edge.

"Oh, God..."

There's mischief in those eyes, and with a final teasing

nip of his teeth against the sensitive bundle of nerves, Seth finally gives in and presses his lips firmly against my throbbing centre. Waves of pleasure crash over me, radiating from that point of contact and spreading throughout my entire body. I grasp for something to hold onto. His tongue dances skillfully, swirling and flicking in a rhythmic motion that drives me to the brink of madness.

I feel myself losing control, surrendering completely to the sensations he's creating. My back arches involuntarily, my hips rising to meet his mouth as he continues to feast on me. The intensity of his ministrations is intoxicating, pushing me further into a realm of pure bliss.

Every stroke of his tongue, every gentle suck sends jolts of electricity through my veins. I am lost in a sea of pleasure, drowning in sensations that leave me breathless and craving more. The outside world fades away as all that exists is this moment.

I am consumed by him—his touch, his taste, his scent filling my senses and overwhelming my every thought.

His tongue dances with an expert grace, tracing patterns of ecstasy along the sensitive folds of my most intimate place. Each flick and stroke builds on the last and I'm on the precipice of a climax that promises to be earth-shattering.

As his lips suck on my swollen nub, my body convulses with electric currents of pleasure. A moan escapes my lips, a primal sound that echoes in the air around us. Seth's fingers slip inside me, their movements matching the rhythm of his skilled tongue. The dual sensations send me spiralling into a vortex of pure sensation.

. . .

I GRIP the sheets beneath me, my knuckles white. Seth's tongue works its magic, exploring every inch of my core with an unyielding hunger.

My body trembles at the exquisite torture he inflicts upon me, my moans growing louder and more desperate with each passing second.

With a final surge of determination, Seth increases the tempo of his movements. His fingers thrust in and out of me, matching the rhythm of his tongue as it flicks and dances over my swollen bud. The pressure within me reaches unbearable heights, pushing me closer and closer to the edge.

I can't hold back any longer. My body tenses, every muscle coils like a spring ready to unleash its power. Sensations explode through me like fireworks, each touch igniting a new burst of pleasure.

"Seth ..."

I gasp his name, my voice a mixture of need and urgency. Seth looks up at me, his eyes smouldering with an intensity that matches my own. He withdraws his fingers from within me, eliciting a whine of loss from deep within my throat.

"I need you," I whisper, my voice barely audible over the pounding of my heart. Seth's lips curve into a wicked smile as he rises to his feet, a predatory gleam in his eyes. He sheds his clothes with deliberate slowness, revealing a body chiselled with strength and desire.

I watch him hungrily, unable to tear my gaze away from the sight before me. His hard muscles ripple with his movements, each flex and stretch a testament to the power he holds. My breathing quickens as he crawls back onto the bed, his eyes never leaving mine.

His lips descend upon my mouth, a searing kiss that

leaves me breathless and wanting. The taste of him reignites a fire deep inside and I pull him to me.

With one easy movement, he slips inside, filling me completely. I gasp, my arms wrapping around him. The sensation is overwhelming, a heady mix of pleasure and need that threatens to consume us both. Each thrust of his hips sends shockwaves of ecstasy through my body.

I LOSE myself in the moment, surrendering to the raw passion that binds us together. Sweat coats our bodies as we move in perfect synchrony, our bodies becoming one in a dance.

There is a tenderness in his touch that takes my breath away. With each thrust, he holds me close, his arms wrapped tightly around my trembling body. His lips find mine again, kissing me with a hunger that mirrors my own.

The room fills with the sounds of our pleasure. Moans and gasps blend together, creating an erotic melody that feeds the intensity of our connection. I can feel the heat building within me once more, a deep ache that only Seth can quench.

As his pace quickens, so does the storm within me. Every stroke of his hardened length pushes me further towards the edge of euphoria. I clench around him, urging him on.

His eyes lock with mine, a silent promise passing between us. The pleasure builds like a tidal wave, threatening to crash upon the shore of my senses and consume me whole. Seth's grip on my hip tightens as he senses my impending climax.

And then it happens. The dam of pleasure breaks, and a

tsunami of ecstasy floods through me, washing away any coherent thought. I arch my back, my body trembling as waves of pleasure crash over me, each one stronger than the last.

"I've got you," he whispers ... those words again.

I swallow hard, feeling those words. "I've got you, too." He moves still, a relentless rhythm, his own desire driving him forward. His brows furrow in concentration, his muscles straining as he inches closer to his own release. I can see the intensity in his eyes. I want to watch him, but my body is lost.

His fingers dig into my flesh, leaving delicious marks on my hips as he thrusts deeper and harder. The sound of our bodies colliding fills the room, punctuated by our echoing gasps and cries of pleasure. Seth's movements become more urgent, his hips slamming into mine with a primal need.

I watch him through half-lidded eyes, devouring the sight of him lost in passion. The way his jaw clenches, his eyes filled with a wild hunger that drives him forward. In this moment, he is both predator and protector, claiming me as his own while cherishing every inch of my trembling body.

AND THEN, with a final thrust, Seth finds his release. A guttural groan escapes his lips as he spills himself inside me, the warmth of his essence flooding my senses. I revel in the raw power of his climax, my body convulsing around him, milking every last drop of pleasure from him.

When he is done and trembling from the aftershocks of our shared ecstasy, he collapses onto me, his weight comforting and familiar. Our bodies glisten with a sheen of sweat as we catch our breath, the air thick with the scent of our passionate union.

I fall asleep in his arms. Sleep takes me and my dreams are light.

Until they're not ...

CHAPTER
FORTY-THREE

The doors swing open abruptly as two vampires escort Jonathan into the room, his resistance evident in the way he shoves and pulls at them. "What the hell is this?" he demands, his voice echoing with indignation, as he's thrust into the main room where Donovan awaits with his book.

Jonathan staggers forward, his balance momentarily lost. He quickly regains his footing and shoots Donovan a glare of fiery determination.

"I asked, what's going on?"

Donovan steps forward, his posture relaxed yet authoritative, like a seasoned businessman ready to close a crucial deal. "Jonathan, Jonathan, Jonathan ..." he coos, almost melodically emphasising his name.

Jonathan's gaze sweeps the room, his alarm growing as he spots Marcus and Amelia. Even to someone unfamiliar with their kind, it's clear these two are predators, akin to cats poised to pounce at the first sign of weakness. In their human lives, Jonathan muses, they were probably cowards, now masquerading as threats.

He instinctively steps back, but says nothing, his silence a testament to his wariness.

"You weren't infected by Alitora," Donovan observes, tilting his head slightly as he scrutinises Jonathan. "Your daughter and wife got sick, but you – you were unscathed."

Jonathan shrugs, feigning indifference. "Maybe I just got lucky. It's the luck of the draw."

Donovan chuckles softly. "Ah, but that's where you're mistaken. It's not luck – it's your genetic makeup, or should I say, the lineage you descend from. Come here, do me a favour."

Jonathan eyes Donovan suspiciously, distrust etched in every line of his face. Despite his apprehension, he cautiously moves closer, his gaze darting between Marcus and Amelia. Marcus stands with his hands clasped behind his back, sporting a sinister smile, reminiscent of a snake poised to strike. Amelia lounges in a chair, her long nails rhythmically tapping on the table's surface.

Approaching the table where the book lies, Jonathan peers down at it. "What is this?"

"A grimoire," Donovan reveals with a hint of satisfaction.

Jonathan narrows his eyes, scepticism mingling with curiosity. "Like a witch's book?"

"Exactly like a witch's book," Donovan confirms. "I need you to open it."

Jonathan furrows his brow in confusion but compiles, his fingers gingerly turning the cover of the grimoire's pages. Donovan watches eagerly, a cloth pressed to his nose, stained with the dark hue of his own blood. His anticipation is thick, his focus singular.

As the pages flutter, a brilliant light bursts forth, illuminating the words written in a long-forgotten script. Donovan's eyes light up with triumph. "Yes ... This is it," he murmurs.

But the light and the words fade as quickly as they appeared, disappearing like sparks in a dark room. Donovan's elation turns to frustration. "No. Fucking no." He snatches the book back, desperately flipping through the pages, searching for the words.

Jonathan takes a step back, eager to distance himself from the volatile situation.

"What the fucking hell ..." Donovan mutters under his breath.

In a swift, unexpected move, Donovan grabs Jonathan's wrist, his grip ironclad. He slashes across Jonathan's bare skin with his nail, drawing blood effortlessly. Jonathan struggles, but the vampire's centuries-old strength is overwhelming.

Donovan turns Jonathan's hand, letting the blood drip onto the book's cover. The cover absorbs the blood greedily, as if starved for it. The book flares to life again, but the words remain elusive, fading as soon as they appear.

Meeting Jonathan's eyes, Donovan shakes his head in frustration. "It's Payton we need. Payton's blood. But your blood ... your blood holds the power."

Jonathan's eyes widen with fear, a deep, visceral terror that grips him. He attempts to pull away, but Donovan's grasp is unyielding.

Donovan positions Jonathan closer, his hands firm on the man's temples. The need to feed, to quell the pounding in his head from the relentless sun outside, is overpowering.

He manoeuvres Jonathan, securing his grip, then tilts his head to expose the vulnerable neck. Jonathan's heart pounds wildly, his breathing ragged with fear.

As Donovan's lips brush the nape of Jonathan's neck, a shiver of dread runs through him. The scent of his fear is intoxicating to Donovan, fueling his primal need.

With a powerful surge, Donovan sinks his fangs into the soft flesh of Jonathan's neck. A sharp pain courses through him, intermingling with a bewildering rush of pleasure. The sensation is overwhelming, a maelstrom of agony and ecstasy unlike anything he has ever known.

Donovan feeds voraciously on Jonathan's lifeblood, feeling the hot rush of vitality invigorate every part of him. With each draw, he senses an increase in his power and vitality, a resurgence of life coursing through his veins.

For Jonathan, reality blurs into a hazy mist as he succumbs to the overpowering sensation of the fangs buried in his neck. The rhythmic drawing of his blood transforms the room into a disorienting whirl of colours and emotions. Time loses its grip, and pain melds into an eerie pleasure, a vampire's deceptive gift. But Donovan's true intent lies elsewhere; he's delving deep into Jonathan's mind, searching for the latent magic.

And there it is, just as Marcus had said - dormant, yet unmistakably present. Jonathan, unbeknownst to himself, is a conduit for Payton, a carrier of her inherited magic. Donovan can feel the faint thread, the subtle connection between father and daughter.

"Find her," he urges through their mental link. "Where is she?"

Jonathan's mind, under Donovan's forceful guidance, reaches out like a beacon. His thoughts, manipulated by Donovan, plead desperately. "Help me," he thinks, his silent plea travelling down the psychic connection to the daughter he let go.

He finds her in the ethereal plane of the mind, asleep

yet reachable. Donovan skillfully weaves images of Jonathan in distress, in need of his daughter's aid.

"Help me, Payton," he whispers into her subconscious. "Help me."

In her mind's eye, Payton sees her father, a lone figure in an empty space. "Dad?" she questions, her voice tinged with uncertainty.

Donovan, manipulating Jonathan's image, urges him forward, making him a puppet to his will. "Please …" Jonathan's avatar pleads.

Payton's eyes widen, her stance guarded. "What's wrong?"

Jonathan's figure crumbles, feigning despair. "I'm so sorry … I'm sorry. Please." He shakes his head. "I had to do it. I … They controlled me. I had to send you away. I tried to keep you safe. Out of their way."

As he speaks of Seth's alleged intentions, of having to hide her for her safety, Donovan orchestrates every move, every tear. Jonathan's avatar falls to his knees, a picture of remorse and desperation.

He can hear her heart beating. "I don't understand."

He shakes his head. "They're dangerous, Payton. They';re worse than we ever knew. I …" He glances over his shoulder, as if looking at something, but there is nothing there on this plain. "He's coming. He …"

Payton hesitates, her heart torn. "Dad, please …"

"You have to help me. I can't … they …" He puts his hands to his face and sobs. "Help me. I …"

In her mind, she goes to him, falling to her knees beside him. She's wavering, her longing for paternal love and forgiveness clouding her judgement. Donovan silently rejoices, his plan unfolding perfectly.

Jonathan reaches for her, his body trembling.

"Tell me what you need."

"To escape. We can leave together, you and I …" He lets out a whimper.

Payton's resolve slips. She reaches for her father. "Get to St. Mary's Hospital by next light and wait for me there," she instructs.

Jonathan weeps, nodding. "I love you so much. I always have."

Her eyes fill, she nods. "I love you too."

In the real world, Donovan releases Jonathan, the connection severed. He steps back, watching as Jonathan slumps, drained and disoriented. Donovan's eyes glint with triumph, his scheme set in motion.

The End

Season Four Coming Soon

DID YOU ENJOY THAT?

I love hearing from my readers and I love connecting with them.
Please remember to leave me a review too. Reviews are so important to us authors. Even if all you can say is, damn that book was amazing ... then that is fine with me.
Thank you so much.

PLACES TO FIND ME

Email me - masonsabre2@gmail.com
Find me on facebook - https://www.facebook.com/msabre3
Website – Authormasonsabre.com
My author page - https://www.facebook.com/AuthorMasonSabre

TEAM SABRE

Wolf Club

Help me to keep these books coming by joining my Patreon. In return, I'll give you exclusive access to chapters before the books are released, a behind the scenes look at my writer life and not published elsewhere short stories.

I also give away advanced copies of books in ebook format before they're released as well as signed paperbacks, hardbacks, mugs, and other merchandise at no extra cost to you. It is all part of your support.

But not just that. You'll be joining an already thriving reader community, where I get to chat with you about the books you love to read.

Support from $3 and you can cancel anytime you like, with no questions. But I'm pretty sure you won't want to.

See you there.

Mason

https://www.patreon.com/masonsabre

Also by Mason Sabre
SOCIETY BOOKS

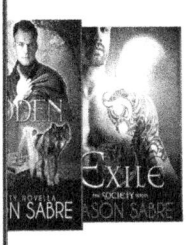

Book 1 Cade

Book 2 Dark Veil

Book 3 Case 36

Book 4 Hidden

Book 5 Fractured

Book 6 Sebastian

Book 7 Exile

Book 8 Broken

Book 9 The Forgotten

Origin story - The Rise of the Phoenix

Origin Story - Henry

Book 10 Moon Night

Book 11 Alpha - Coming soon

Society Companion Books

Death Awakening

Broken Snow

Seraph

Bleed

Chaos

Martial Magic

Enigma

Mortal Wings

Fangliner

Rogue

Other Books by Mason Sabre

Death Dealers (With Rachel Morton)

Dead on Time

Dead on Arrival

Dead on Target

Dead to Me

Skin Trade Series

Blood Slave

Blood Oath

Blood Bond

Others

Watch Over you

Cuts Like an Angel

Cuts like an Angel 2

Cuts Like an Angel 3

Lucy

She Promised

Twisted

Non-Fiction

10,000 Words per Day

Write Better Scenes

Patreon for Writers

Printed in Great Britain
by Amazon